LAND'S END TO JOHN O'GROATS

A photographic journal of our 1,443-mile walk

Meg Pike

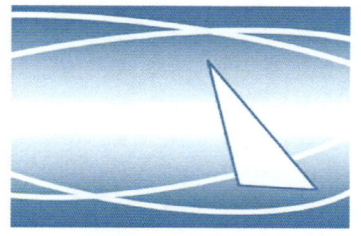

Blue Ocean Publishing

The author and the publisher have taken all reasonable care to ensure that all material in this work is original, or is in the Public Domain, or is used with the permission of the original copyright owners. However, if any person believes that material for which they own the copyright has found its way into this work without permission, they should contact the author, via the publisher, who will seek to investigate and remedy any inadvertent infringement.

Land's End to John O'Groats: A photographic journal of our 1,443-mile walk
© Meg Pike 2016

The right of Meg Pike to be identified as the author of this work has been asserted by her in accordance with the Copyright, Designs and Patents Act 1988. All rights reserved. No part of this publication may be reproduced, stored in a retrieval system or transmitted in any form or by any means, electronic, mechanical, photocopying, recording, scanning, or otherwise, without prior written permission of the copyright holder.

Published by Blue Ocean Publishing St John's Innovation Centre
Cambridge CB4 0WS United Kingdom

http://www.blueoceanpublishing.biz

A catalogue record for this book is available from the British Library.

ISBN 978-1-907527-31-9

First published in the United Kingdom in 2016 by Blue Ocean Publishing.

LAND'S END TO JOHN O'GROATS

A PHOTOGRAPHIC JOURNAL OF OUR 1,443 MILE WALK

July 2011: Land's End to Bath
using parts of the **Macmillan Way** and also the **Camel Trail**

October 2011: Bath to Chipping Campden
walking **The Cotswold Way**

July 2012: Chipping Campden to Malham Tarn
including **The Heart of England Way**
Staffordshire Way (part)
The Pennine Way (part 1)

October 2012: Malham Tarn to Cow Green Reservoir
on **The Pennine Way (part 2)**

July 2013: Cow Green Reservoir to the Falkirk Wheel
walking the Final section of **The Pennine Way** (part 3)
to Kirk Yetholm
St Cuthbert's Way (Kirk Yetholm to Melrose)
and part of the **Southern Uplands Way.**
Footpaths to reach Union Canal
and on to The Falkirk Wheel and the Forth and Clyde Canal

May 2014: The Falkirk Wheel to Findhorn Bridge, Tomatin
walking to Milngavie
West Highland Way to Fort William
East Highland Way to Aviemore
Burma Road to near Carrbridge,
and on to Findhorn Bridge at Tomatin

May 2015: Findhorn Bridge to John O'Groats
(no public rights of way on the maps in Scotland)

HOW IT ALL CAME ABOUT

Meet two couples: Bob and Lynne, and Meg and Andy (plus dog: Zak and Dexter respectively).

We'd met in 2005 when Andy and I joined the Home Counties Folk Dance and Song Section of the Camping and Caravanning Club. On the various rallies we attended Bob regularly led walks, and Andy and I, also being keen walkers, would go along.

Andy, Bob, Lynne and Meg with Dexter the dog

In 2007, Bob and Lynne undertook and completed Wainwright's Coast to Coast Walk. We walked the Coast to Coast the following year in 2008 (backpacking) with my sister Mary and her daughter Martha: then 12 years old. So here was a walking experience that Andy and I had in common with Bob and Lynne.

In 2009, Bob suggested that we might like to join them to walk Offa's Dyke: using both cars, (one each end of the sections of walk) and staying in our caravans, moving site when necessary. We weren't sure how this would work out but were keen to try it. So in July 2009 we set off. Well, we were still friends after two weeks of walking and socialising together, and we were fairly evenly matched as far as walking speed and abilities. We had a great holiday.

Towards the end of 2009, I received an email from Bob – 'How about Land's End to John O' Groats for our next project?' Thinking he was joking, I replied back, 'Why not, When shall we start?'

Bob's reply showed me that this was no joke!! His plan was for us to walk on footpaths, as far as possible, from Land's End to John O' Groats: this would require much planning of both route and sites for our caravans for the entire length of the walk. So, there was to be much planning in 2010 (and a chance for Lynne to have what she referred to as 'a proper holiday first') before we were to set off on our adventure in July 2011.

The Practicalities of the task in hand.

In effect, the walk, **Land's End to John O' Groats,** known as **'LeJog'**, would be split into seven parts: Three weeks in July 2011, one week in October 2011, three weeks walking in July 2012 with a further week in October of that same year, three weeks in July 2013, four weeks in May 2014, and finally, another four weeks in May 2015. There would be some days when we didn't walk, as we had to move the caravans on to new sites.

What I didn't know, before we started this great adventure, was that there was no 'official route' from Land's End to John O' Groats (or vice versa). Many have road walked, making use of the A9 as they headed towards John O' Groats, others have walked the coastal path through Cornwall and Devon, then used Offa's Dyke, Pennine Way, and their own routes through Scotland (some heading up the east coast, others taking the western routes over mountainous terrain, to reach their goal.)

There is no defined right way to go. There were, we found, a few books on other walkers' experiences and routes, which we looked at and either took on board or discarded due to length of walk day, or difficulty in placing a car each end of the day's walking, as we planned to do.

There was much pleasure involved in the planning: poring over maps and books, and matching our walking route to be near suitable caravan sites, as much as we could. We had already decided that we wanted our route to be scenic, to enjoy the countryside around us, and to avoid main roads.

It was agreed that Bob and Andy would plan alternate 'three week' sections of the walk: Bob taking on the first section, from Land's End to reach Bath. All planning was looked at together, and agreed upon by the four of us. This necessitated a good many meetings and many a meal at each other's houses, and our friendship grew stronger as a result. We had fun planning. There was a growing sense of achievement as we planned and progressed north. There was also much trepidation, especially from Lynne and myself, when the men suggested that we walk the whole of the Pennine Way as part of the route. Having read Wainwright's dismal portrayal of this route: of the bogs and peat, and mile upon mile of barren moorland, we weren't at all sure we were up to this. However, we were persuaded. Bob and Andy's enthusiasm for this eventually rubbed off on us. I think it was Bob's eagerness to see 'High Cup Nick' that clinched it!!

As part of the route it was decided that we would walk The West Highland Way to Fort William, and if Andy could plan the route to take us near The Falkirk Wheel on the way to Milngavie, so much the better. We had thought we might use The Great Glen Way, but as the walk evolved we decided on a new route: The East Highland Way, which would take us to Aviemore.

From Aviemore we would work our way north, heading for the east coast of Scotland beyond Inverness. Planning routes in Scotland was more difficult as there are no public footpaths marked on the maps up here. We made use of some of the suggestions in the guide books we had resourced, and by the time we reached John O' Groats we had walked a total of 1443 miles, over 112 walk days.

The Realities

There was a routine to each day that went something like this:

Wake up 6.30 am (or if we were lucky 7 am)
8 – 8.30 am: drive to position vehicles ready to start the walk, leaving one car at the walk end.
Walking by 9 am (or as near as possible, dependent upon length of journey to leave vehicles)
Finish walking around 4 pm
Back to collect car (when needed) and travel to site
If really unlucky – much boot cleaning!!
Load photographs on to laptop and list photos
Write up the 'log' for the day's walk
Much needed cup (s) of tea and showers
Evening meal (either in caravan, or, if fortunate, a meal at a nearby pub)
Meet up to discuss next day's walk
Prepare packed lunches
Early (-ish) to bed to be up in time for tomorrow's walk

Every fourth or fifth day, we would move site, also taking advantage of this day to buy food supplies and for washing clothes.

The other realities were that the countryside we were walking through was often far from any access to facilities, and quite often, even when we hoped for refreshment as we passed through villages and towns, we were disappointed to find cafes and pubs closed, or no longer there.

The saying goes 'No pain, no gain'. In this instance it was relatively little pain, for greater gain.

Walking Land's End to John O' Groats has been one of the most rewarding experiences in my life and it has given me a heartfelt appreciation of the beautiful landscapes we have in the British Isles.

From the more intimate landscapes through to the grand view: together with our agricultural heartlands and towns and cities along the way, all have contributed to give me a real understanding of the geography of the country we have walked through and explored.

We made use of our walk to appreciate the scenery, to think about the history of the different places we went through, occasionally stopping to look inside a church as we passed, and to enjoy our walk: and whatever the weather, there was always a scene to admire along the way.

The many and diverse wild flowers, attractive villages, picturesque lochs and lakes: all competed with the impressive vastness of the moorland and hillside views to be photographed. It became for me a journey of photographic opportunities, that I would never experience again.

This is why my journal has been based upon the photographic, rather than the text. Although the text is important: it describes the day, and my outlook upon it, and is of value in this regard, it soon became clear to me that the photos I took served as a greater reminder of the experience, and it is for this reason that this journal has taken the form it now has.

There was a great sense of camaraderie that developed between Bob and Lynne, and Andy and me, and I am so grateful to Bob that he suggested that we undertake this challenge. Yes, there were problems that we encountered along the way and things didn't always go to plan, but we overcame these problems together.

Therefore, it was with very mixed emotions that we finished the walk in 2015. We had so enjoyed the experience that we were reluctant for it to end, but we were also overwhelmed by the fact that we had completed the challenge.

We are even now planning the next walk together, but I don't believe that any walk could surpass our Land's End to John O' Groats expedition for its variety of landscape and beauty of countryside. Time will tell!

THE START OF THE WALK

'LEJOG'

THE FOUR OF US AT LAND'S END

(Andy, Meg, Bob and Lynne, and dog, Zak)

SUNDAY 10TH JULY 2011

Day 1   Sunday 10th July 2011   Land's End to Gulval Church   15.2 miles

The important day had arrived: and with excitement, anticipation and just a touch of trepidation, we arrived in Bob's car at Gulval Church, just outside Penzance, where we had a taxi to Land's End. On arrival at Land's End we found we could register that we were starting 'LeJog' today, by signing in at the hotel, and after taking our 'start of walk' photos *the walk* began.

A look back to Long Ship's Lighthouse

Andy, Bob and Lynne on Coast Path

The start of the walk took us along the coast path to Sennen Cove – across the very sandy beach – quite hard going to walk along. However we had much to look at as we made our way to the far end of the beach: the view to Sennen harbour, the coastal path ahead, and out in the sea were several groups of surfers receiving tuition. Near the end of the beach we turned off the coastal path – which though very pleasant – would have been a long and convoluted route for us.

Surfers at Sennen Cove

Evening primroses and the cottages after Sennen Cove

Instead, we walked inland, up above the Cove and past cottages, with beautiful displays of evening primroses. We were heading now to the first highpoint since Land's End: Carn Brea. This hill is the most westerly in Britain. An important landmark: the bronze age summit cairn of a type found only in Scilly and West Cornwall. In the medieval period, a hermitage and chapel stood here, giving the hill its name. The beacon is still lit every midsummer eve.

As we reached the top of this cairn it clouded over, but we found a sheltered spot to have our lunch. From Carn Brea we took the path down towards Carn Euny (an ancient Romano-British settlement) passing an interestingly painted house with a dragon on each end. We were now in an area where there were mine shafts around, and signs to that effect.

Chapel Carn Brea (and the painted house)

On reaching the ancient settlement of Carn Euny there was much to see of the former village. We explored this for a little while before carrying on our way.

One of the 'tunnels' at Carn Euny

Part of the site of the ancient village of Carn Euny

On towards the hamlet of Grumbla and a little bit of road walking to the village of Sancreed, where we came upon the '*Pig Walk*' – people dressed up and carrying a *large pink model pig* through the village – a very festive scene.

Pig Walk at Sancreed

After Sancreed we reached Sellan across farmland, and near a reservoir. More farmland and slightly obscure footpaths – signage was a bit of a problem at various points today: one farm earlier today had a sign which said 'Keep to way-marked path' but there were no way marks!! We had to retrace our steps a couple of times or so today.

We carried on around land belonging to Trengwainton House to the village of Madron, where we stopped in a pleasant remembrance garden for a drink and flapjack. More 'tricky' map reading for Bob as we made our way across more farmland to Gulval Church. There were many granite stone stiles: large blocks of stone placed horizontally: Quite difficult to negotiate at times – being quite high up and steep down.

Footpath walking across arable fields: the track across has been made clear here

It became quite warm and sunny this afternoon and generally the weather was good today. A little bleak and grey at Land's End, but as we progressed inland there was more varied landscape and many wild flowers. Pretty gardens occasionally with palm trees and colourful flowers.

By the time we reached Gulval, and Bob's waiting car, we had walked 15.2 miles.

Bob and Andy taking their boots off outside Gulval Church (and Zak)

Day 2   Monday 11th July 2011   Gulval Church to Knave-Go-By   21.1 miles

From Gulval Church we took the path to Penzance and then along the South West Coastal Path to Marazion. At Marazion we decided to detour and cross the causeway to St. Michael's Mount. Lynne and I bought postcards. Meanwhile Bob and Andy had noticed that the tide was starting to come in, so we made a hasty exit from the island: safely reaching the mainland (but not without going through a few inches of sea-water on the way!) Stopped for coffee in Marazion where we had a good view of the now rapidly flooding causeway.

From Marazion we walked northwards on good paths for several miles. Missed a path briefly but soon got back on track: a good wide path through some heathland and old mine workings, eventually passing some fir trees and arriving at at a road.

Lynne at wooded section of path before the road

Took the road for a while, and we were going well today until we got to an impenetrable patch of woodland where the path should be! After exploring other options, without success, we eventually had to retrace our steps half a mile or so to then take an alternative route which meant another two miles added to today's walk. This was just to the south of Hayle. We had lunch in a green field off the lane, and eventually joined our original route further on. Some difficult paths later in the afternoon, busy roads, electric fences, cavorting cows – Zak caught one of the electric fences and yelped – poor Zak! Two hours later than planned we arrived at Leedstown and we stopped for a welcome ice-cream before continuing across fields, a mixture of barley, wheat, linseed: some with good signage, some definitely not.

A couple of times today we had to rely on compass bearings and GPS readings to get the footpath line across crops, where no visible path had been left.

Stopped at the site of an ancient burial stone or 'quoit', and had a 'flapjack' stop for energy boost. We were quite tired by now and, without stopping to explore the 'quoit', we carried on along the final 2.5 miles to the old mine workings at Knave-Go-By: just south of Cambourne, and arrived at our waiting car.

A good path toward Knave-Go-By

Nearing the end of today's walk

We'd walked 21.1 miles today and we were pleased to find a fish and chip shop in Beacon where we bought our supper: eating this in the car in the nearby station car park. We were very tired and stiff as we got out of the car and we arrived back at site just before 9 pm!

Day 3   **Tuesday 12th July 2011**   **Knave-Go-By to Langarth**   **15 miles**

Just a ten-minute bus ride to Pool to rejoin the route for today's walk. At Pool there was a restored beam engine, *National Trust*, but not open to the public today: however we could have a look at the outside of it.

Engine House - Pool (Bob exploring)

From there a bit of road walking to get to where we'd walked to yesterday, and back to the old mine engine housings we'd seen previously.

Old engine housings near Brea

Our first destination today was the hill 'Carn Brea' (the same name as the hill on Day 1) which was about 4 or 5 miles distant, and we could see it ahead of us. Aiming for the rocky outcrop at the top of this hill: a bit like a 'tor', we found there was a large monument at the top – very imposing: a four-sided tapering column of granite in memory of a local dignitary, and partway down the other side a 'castle-style' building, which was built over a rocky crag. Also at the top was a very unusually weathered stone.

Andy explores the 'tor' at Carn Brea

Approaching the monument on Carn Brea

Weathered stone - Carn Brea

We had a short break at the top of Carn Brea to admire the views (mainly over the mining town of Cambourne) before heading down through high bracken and a few brambles to a wider track. We were now headed toward Chasewater Valley and followed one of the mining trails for a while until we reached the village of Twelveheads. On the way we passed various relics of the copper mining industry around Cambourne. At one old quarry site there was an outdoor theatre – made from the natural stone of the quarry and some granite blocks set in a semi-circle for the audience.

We stopped there for lunch – the acoustics were amazingly good! On past more evidence of mining in previous century and beyond – quite an alien landscape now. After a short sit-down at Twelvehead we made our way up and out of this pretty valley and over and down to the next valley, then ascending once again to get to Threemilestone. A short walk from there to site where we arrived in good time today – around 4pm. Time for a shower and dinner before a game of whist at Bob and Lynne's caravan. Also discussed, and agreed, to make the next two days walks into three shorter length walks. We'll move on a day later than planned.

| Day 4 | Wednesday 13th July 2011 | Langarth to Mitchell | 12.2 miles |

Walked out from the campsite today going down a lovely wooded lane. We then had to follow a footpath which started out as rather overgrown, but then suddenly was much worse with a mass of nettles about 12 feet deep and wide across the path. Bob drew the short straw here (he had trousers rather than shorts) and went first trampling down the overgrowth. Andy followed behind, stamping the undergrowth down.

Bob trampling down the nettles

When we finally got through we were in an old packhorse lane

and once there we were on a good path, up to a farm, then to a road. Then it was mainly farmland with the terrain being more hilly as we approached lunchtime.

Towards Mitchell we were higher up and there was a bigger landscape ahead: across to the China Clay workings to the south, and ahead of us was the A30 scarring its way through the countryside toward Bodmin.

We stopped for a snack (flapjacks) at the top of a hill, then carried on down hill before taking another packhorse way – tree lined, right back to the village of Mitchell where Bob had parked the car this morning, and took the short drive back to site.

Walking into the village of Mitchell

We had walked 12.2 miles today. We arrived back at site around 2.30 pm. Lynne and I went to the Park and Ride and caught a bus into Truro for a look at the Cathedral, and a bit of essential shopping. Back on site after our evening meal Bob and Lynne came over to us to play some music: Bob on guitar, Lynne on concertina and recorder, I played violin, or sang with Andy.

Day 5 **Thursday 14th July 2011** **Mitchell to St Wenn** **14.5 miles**

Started walking at 9.25 am from Mitchell, but then a series of missing footpath signs and blocked paths until we reached St Enoder: we spent at least 30 minutes trying to find a way past / through ditches, undergrowth and barbed wire at one point. Once at St Enoder, we stopped for a drink, and when we left there we had our first footpath direction sign of the day. A few good fields and stiles and then one very wobbly one that Bob and Andy had to hold upright for Lynne and me to get over!

Wobbly footpath stile after St Enoder

A while later, at one farm, we encountered barbed wire on top of farm gates, that we had to open, which wasn't very 'walker friendly'.

Finally we arrived at Indian Queens where we were tempted by AJ's Eats and Treats cafe. We stopped for a cup of tea and a snack before heading out of town toward St Columb and then Ruthven – a lovely village where we stopped to eat our lunch (sat on a low wall in the sunshine).

Zak finds a drinking spot   *Cottage in Ruthven*

Good walking from there in the main (until 1 mile along a busier road) on to Castle Dinas – a hill fort – quite impressive with outer banks and ditches still very intact. Excellent views to be had from there – to our next destination, Bodmin, to the east and a 360 degrees panoramic view over Cornwall.

Hill fort – Castle Dinas

We found a sheltered spot for flapjack stop (last one) It was lovely and sunny and we spent a good 10-15 minutes enjoying lazing in the sun before leaving the fort on, to begin with, a good path downhill past a bank of rosebay willowherb set against a panoramic view to the sea (northwards), some ponies grazing and a wide path, but then the path narrowed along a field edge, with barbed wire and brambles slowing our progress.

Lazing in the sun at Castle Dinas

On through better paths (but one bull in a cow field) back up to St Wenn, where Bob's car was parked. Back to Mitchell to collect our car to journey to site. We paid our site fees and had our LeJog forms signed. To Bob and Lynne this evening to plan tomorrow.

Day 6 **Friday 15th July 2011** **St Wenn to Helland Bridge** **9.6 miles**

Drove to St Wenn. The first footpath we wanted couldn't be found, so we road walked for a while. A mixture today of footpaths and lanes, some footpaths were very good – mown grass, wide and well signed – others definitely were not, but apart from the first footpath we had no real problems today. Good views towards Bodmin Moor – prettier countryside now generally.

Approaching the church in Withiel

Went through Withiel and on to Nanstanton, and the start of the Camel Trail. Stopped at a pub for coffee / hot chocolate before walking a 'good pace' (set by the men) down the Camel Trail alongside the River Camel to Helland Bridge.

The River Camel from the Camel Trail

While waiting for our taxi back to St Wenn, we had our picnic lunch and arrived back at St Wenn by about 2.30 pm. We drove back to site at Langarth, where we had a cup of tea before getting 'ready to roll' to our next campsite at Lifton. Set up camp and then drove to Launceston for supplies. Back to the village of Lifton for a pub meal to end the day. The site at Lifton is very convenient, being close to our walking route, but not as lovely as the one at Langarth with its wonderful views.

Day 7   Saturday 16th July 2011   Helland Bridge to near Trebray   18.7 miles

We had firstly 3.5 miles of continuing along the Camel Trail to Penpont, where we saw advertised (three times) a teashop, but when we arrived at Penpont there was a sign saying "SORRY, CLOSED TODAY": a real shame as we were quite looking forward to tea and cakes by then!!

Fine drizzle on and off to begin with. Coats on and off as the rain became heavier. On to St Breward and then up to Bodmin Moor. Gorse bushes and short grazed grass, foxgloves and other heathland flowers. Lane walking at first and then off on a track heading over the moor toward 'Brown Willy' (highest point on the moor). We saw horses and hounds at the start of this section.

Horses and Hounds on Bodmin Moor

Crossed a road by a 'finger post' and walked over to a wooden bench for a drink stop. We were there only a very short while before very heavy rain arrived. On with the waterproofs again: speedily, and we carried on walking across the moor. Open moorland for a while, cattle, horses and sheep grazing, then through a belt of fir trees and down hill where we found a sheltered spot for lunch, with a lovely view across the valley and to the stream below (the rain had eased by now). The route then took us along to an abandoned stone cottage at which the path went downhill to the stream and then uphill. We carried on up over the moor until we reached the trig point at the top of Brown Willy. Very windy as we walked along the ridge to the top, but great views to the sea (North Cornwall) and across the county. Views to Dartmoor and Devon to the east.

Rough Tor (on our left as we climbed up to Brown Willy)

Down from Brown Willy over moorland, and then up and over Butten Hill (on a compass bearing), gradually losing height until we reached grassland and gorse bushes as we arrived at the lower levels.

The view as we came down from Butten Hill

Along the edge of the moor along a track, and then a road, passing a lovely old stone bridge by a ford, where Zak met a 'friend'.

Andy at the old stone bridge, with Zak and his 'new friend';

Walking from there along the lanes back to reach the car near Trebay, the banks on either side were a mass of wild flowers.

Day 8   **Sunday 17th July 2011**   **Near Trebray to Lifton**   **18.01 miles**

We started walking from near Trebray, walking along lanes toward the Rising Sun Pub: mainly lane walking until we reached Launceston. The countryside is prettier now, with very green pastureland and rolling hills. The hedgerows are full of different wild flowers: meadowsweet, honeysuckle, rosebay willowherb, foxgloves, various types of cow parsley, ragged robin, yellow and purple vetch, herb robert, pink campion – to name but a few.

Walked down the Inny Valley and back up the other side, with the River Inny flowing very well after last night's rain! (and today's) and it was an interesting bridge it flowed under. Uphill from there – a very pretty valley.

It was showery all day today, some heavy, but there were dry spells in between. After nine miles or so we came across New Mills Farm Park, which had a cafe. We stopped for a 'hot chocolate', sitting under cover, but outside, escaping the frequent showers. Next to the Farm Park was the last station on the Launceston Valley Railway. We went up to the platform and found a seat, again under cover, where we could sit and eat lunch (and dodge the rain). While we were there the 1.20 pm steam train arrived and we took photos and chatted to the 'lady' train driver.

Steam Train at New Mills Farm Park

Then back on with the walk along the road into Launceston itself, going into the Town Centre: town square, castle and town hall. Sunday today and so there were no shops open here (unlike some parts of the UK).

After a little confusion over finding the start of the Two Castles Way, we set off on this route: which links Launceston and Okehampton, as far as Lifton, and our campsite. The Two Castles Way crossed the River Tamar at Polson Bridge, the border between Devon and Cornwall. Andy was now looking forward to walking through his home county, and with the hope of good footpaths ahead.

Andy, (Devon born-and-bred) happy at being in Devon

We arrived at site at 5pm: we'd walked 18.1 miles today, having set off walking at 9.30 am this morning. We've now covered 124 miles since Land's End and are in Devon.

Day 9   **Monday 18th July 2011**   **Lifton to Sourton**   **16.5 miles**

Still following the Two Castles Way it was road walking at first into Lifton to then cross a cow field to a bridge. Through further fields *(we couldn't quite find the sign here, but found it eventually)* along bridleways, and tracks through woodland. Quite showery this morning, which meant keeping coats on. Some lane walking to cross the River Thrushel and more country lanes to Stowford. A mixture of country lanes, field and tracks and some *very definite 'ups' and 'downs'* today.

Cows watching: after following us across a large field

We stopped for lunch break in the porch of St Peter's Church, Lew Trenchard: the burial place of the Revd. Sabine Baring-Gould – who wrote the words of the hymn 'Onward Christian Soldiers' and the tune of 'Now the day is over'.

It was raining quite steadily then, as our route took us on the northern edge of the Dartmoor foothills, but there were still some good views to the moor and back toward Launceston – obscured by low cloud and rain at times.

View through trees towards Dartmoor

Our path took us across low moorland and round Burley Wood, with its rocky paths through woodland, and on to the village of Bridestowe (where the pub had just closed after lunch! No hot drink again today – and so we made do with a cold drink from the village shop).

Footpath through Burley Wood

Characterful pub in Sourton

Road walking and then some very wet fields in the persistent rain toward the village of Sourton. A large patch of tall bracken and rosebay willowherb on the path made sure that we were *thoroughly wet* at the end of the walk!! However, another 16.5 miles done today.

Day 10   Tuesday 19th July 2011   Sourton to Okehampton   5.9 miles

We moved site from Lifton to Chittlehamholt – the new site is lovely, with views out across the valley. The site owners very friendly and welcoming with a cup of tea and biscuits on our arrival. A rather narrow lane on the way to site with passing places caused a bit of a problem: two cars had to 'back up' the road until we passed them, and it was very steeply uphill.

Once on site we had lunch before setting off to Okehampton to catch the 2.30 pm bus to Sourton, where the walk finished yesterday. Better weather today – a couple of light showers and that was all – better visibility too. From Sourton we walked *up* to the moor toward Sourton Tor from the Sourton Parish sign. There were good views to be had back across to yesterday's route and of Dartmoor to our right. Good walking on grassy paths, the hillside grazed by sheep between the bracken. Across the moor to a pleasant grassy lane – excellent walking – and views to our right of High Willhays. The path gradually descended to a stony path leading to Meldon.

Up onto Dartmoor

Sourton Tor

We took a short detour to look at the iron viaduct before carrying on our route over the East Okement river, crossing this on a wooden bridge, then heading uphill to cross the A30.

Crossing the Okement River

Then across moorland and a golf course to reach Okehampton Castle, from where we took the Tarka Trail through the town, back to our waiting car.

Arriving at Okehampton

Back to site at Chittlehamholt, and a meal at the nearby Exeter Inn. *(Very good.)*

Day 11   Wednesday 20th July 2011   Okehampton to Iddesleigh   13.1 miles

From Okehampton we rejoined the Tarka Trail, heading uphill out of the town. At the top of that section was a good view back over the town.

View from the Tarka Trail down to Okehampton

From there downhill on a lane and then left on a forestry track, and more uphill. Through the woodland for a while and then it was lane walking to Jacobstowe and on towards Hatherleigh. *(A couple of young foxhounds joined us for quite a while and it took Bob much persuading them to return home.)* After quite a few miles of road walking – weather dry now, although still quite cloudy, we went across three sheep fields to Hatherleigh, which is a very picturesque, historic and quaint, small town / large village.

Hatherleigh

Fountain in Hatherleigh

Stopped at a cafe, 'Cornucopia', for coffee (served by two very pleasant gentlemen) and shortly afterwards made another stop in the market square: near a bakers' shop, which Bob couldn't resist, to have our lunch. We also took some time to explore the nearby church, where there was a beautiful stained glass window.

Stained Glass Window in Hatherleigh Church

Continuing our walk we headed out of the town and across a 'cut' hayfield back to the Tarka Trail. It was warmer now with the sun coming through at last. Good green fields, rolling countryside: here and beyond. Several cow fields, then some woodland and more pasture land to reach Iddesleigh church and the car.

Countryside as we approach Iddesleigh

Day 12   **Thursday 21st July 2011**   **Iddesleigh to Chittlehamholt**   **14.4 miles**

Drove to Iddesleigh. A fine sunny day, so a pleasant day for walking. From the pretty village of Iddesleigh we took footpaths to Dolton where we had coffee / hot chocolate at the Rams Head Inn. It was very pleasant to sit outside in the sunshine. From Dolton we made good time (4.1 mph) along the lanes. Then we were on footpaths, through fields and woods, with many ups and downs. Some paths were a little difficult with undergrowth hampering our progress.

The scenery today was beautiful, especially so in the sunshine. We had good views back to Dartmoor and also ahead to Exmoor. We had a fabulous spot at the top of a grassy field for our lunch stop, with panoramic views of the way we'd come. A mix of lane and field walking took us down to the river, three miles from Chittlehamholt. Much undulating countryside – not much flat ground today. From the river it was a 2.5 miles walk uphill to the ridge where the village of Chittlehamholt is situated, then a walk through the golf course. A couple more fields and we came out on the lane, 50 yards or so from the site. Still sunny! A really good day's walking today and excellent weather.

Photos: (Top left) Walking through flower meadows before lunch. (Top right) Panoramic views towards Chittlehamholt. (Bottom left) The beautiful site at Chittlehamholt. (Bottom right) One of the site's resident 'very relaxed' gnomes.

Day 13   **Friday 22nd July 2011**   **Chittlehamholt to Brayford**   **15.8 miles**

Left at 9.10 am from site, lane walking at first to George Nymphton – the weather getting progressively wetter and we were forced to stop and put coats on.

'Mirror' picture on lane towards George Nymphton

Corn Stooks near South Molton

After George Nymphton a little more lane walking before reaching a footpath heading downhill across a stubble field and then across a stream and up through a cornfield. Onto a lane, passing fields of stooked corn for thatching, and then we had our first view of South Molton.

South Molton in sight

For the next couple of miles we endured heavy rain: and it was *four very wet people and one extremely wet dog* that arrived at a cafe for coffee in South Molton. We decided we deserved cake as well today!

After this pleasant break the rain had thankfully eased and we walked *uphill* out of the town to cross the A361 and continue *uphill* for a while further, on a quiet lane.

Coming over the top of this hill were good views ahead: and it was a pretty lane with rosebay willowherb both sides. We eventually found a spot to sit and have lunch, on a bank just past a river bridge.

Rosebay willow herb along the lane after South Molton

A little more lane walking to join the MacMillan Way West, and the Tarka Trail, alongside the river Bray: very muddy here after this morning's rainfall. We followed the river until we reached and crossed the main road, and then it was *very definitely steeply uphill* on Barton Lane: a rocky path that went on for ever, and always uphill, relentlessly steep for quite a way. However we were eventually rewarded with views, albeit to the quarry far below. Downhill then, thankfully, and a chance for our 'uphill muscles' to recover, on a track leading to High Bray Church. We had a look at the church and then the path took us steeply down, across fields, to Brayford (and our waiting car). Sunny intervals this afternoon and then dry.

Barton Lane

View of Exmoor as we approach Brayford

Day 14   Saturday 23rd July 2011   **Brayford to Exford**   **15.8 miles**

Steep uphill: road walking at first then field paths out of Brayford, up a long clover field and then uphill once more for some fantastic panoramic views to Dartmoor, Bodmin and the North Devon Coast. It was a lovely sunny day today and, with a light breeze, was perfect for good walking.

Up still further to the top of the hill, and even better views, where we turned left along a lane for a while and it was level going, with even a little bit of downhill, until we reached a path that took us down a beautiful deep valley – but too early for a lunch stop yet!

At the end of the valley we went up again, over moorland now: rough marshy grassland with cattle and sheep grazing. Crossed a road and then we were heading uphill again, eventually reaching a wall / path, which we followed for a while, with good views of the steep valleys of Exmoor ahead. Over the moorland we had views towards Wales, Bristol Channel and the North Devon Coastline.

On reaching the top of the Exe valley we went steeply down (even the footpath sign read that it was *very steep*) to Exe head. More moorland walking until we were on an uphill path, passing Exmoor ponies, to reach the car at Exford.

Day 15 **Sunday 24th July 2011** **Exford to Dunster** **11.2 miles**

We moved site, leaving Chittlehamholt around 8.45 am, to head for our next site at West Quantoxhead, where we arrived just before 10 am. After setting up the caravans we drove to Exford: leaving our car at Dunster Castle. Walking across heather moorland, grass and bracken – quite tough going – there didn't seem to be a clear path, but just after we reached a road there was a good track for the 2.5 miles up to Dunkery Beacon.

Views through the hedge from the track to Dunkery Beacon

There were some good views to the south occasionally through the hedge on our right, and as we gained height the view began to open out to the north and east. Quite hazy / misty today so the views were not as clear as they might otherwise have been, but it was still a great panorama from the top of Dunkery Beacon.

Track down from Dunkery Beacon to the village of Wootton Courtney

A little way down from the Beacon we stopped for lunch break – much needed by this time! Then a good track, stony in places, down for another 2.5 miles, the last section going through a pretty beechwood.

Dunster church

Then on a lane to Wootton-Courtney where, once past the church, the route took us up steeply through a grassy field and then woodland, still climbing steadily, before joining a wide track across woodland to our right and heathland to the north. Good walking here, with developing views to the sea and inland, although flies were persistently annoying for quite a while! We followed the track, passing Minehead far below us on our left, on toward Grabbits Hill. From there the track went

View to the Quantock Hills and West Quantoxhead

steadily down to the medieval town of Dunster. Back to the castle to retrieve our car. Then back to Exford to collect Bob's car. We took the coast road A39 down Porlock Hill. Terrific views here of moor and sea.

Day 16   Monday 25th July 2011   Dunster to West Quantoxhead   15.6 miles

From Dunster, where we stopped to admire and take photos of the historic town, we left the town by Gallox bridge and ford, passing a stream to the watermill (where Zak took advantage of a good long drink). Walking up through Dunster Park, mainly woodland, the path was easily lost here but after a brief diversion we reached the earth works of the hill fort Bat's Castle, and were rewarded with fine views. *The men also had a view of a naked tent camper who very quickly retreated into his tent.*

Bob and Andy at the top of Bat's Castle

From there a mix of woodland and hill top walking toward Withycombe Hill – downland meadows and fantastic views down toward the east and to the Quantock Hills, the seaside town of Watchet, and the coast further east.

Rosebay willowherb

View from Withycombe Hill towards the Quantock Hills

Downhill to the village of Withycombe, with its white church. Across farmland to the town of Williton, then across fields toward the Quantock Hills and Bicknoller Hill. Up part of Bicknoller Hill and then west along a hillside path: with good views back along today's section of the walk: as far back as Dunkery Beacon. Through lanes back to site at West Quantoxhead.

Heading towards the Quantock Hills

Day 17   Tuesday 26th July 2011   West Quantoxhead to North Petherton   16.0 miles

Bicknoller Hill was the start of today's walk and it was a long uphill trek, between bracken, on a grassy track. Not too steep, but quite relentlessly up. We were rewarded with fantastic views back towards Minehead and Dunkery Beacon as we climbed. Up to two trig points on the Quantock Hills. Beautiful clear and sunny day so fabulous views all around *(many photos taken here)*.

Down from Lyddeard Hill to a lane through a beech tree avenue, past Great and Narrow Hill, then out to an uphill track through bracken before heading downhill once again through woodland and then up to our final viewpoint today, where we had lunch.

Lunch stop view

Down off the Quantock Hills through cornfields to then walk along country lanes. We stopped at the National Trust owned 'Fyne Court', where there was a tea room – but, to our dismay, after making a bit of a detour to get there, it wasn't open on Tuesdays!! So after a short sit-down we made our way to King's Cliff Wood and Quarry from where we were on field paths and minor roads to the village of North Petherton.

Coming down from the Quantock Hills

Cafe closed!

but a chance to sit down for a while

Day 18   Wednesday 27th July 2011   North Petherton to Catcott   10.8 miles

Left our site at West Quantoxhead to drive to our fifth campsite, at Clewer near Cheddar, before starting our walk today from North Petherton.

Bob and Lynne's car had problems – black smoke coming from the exhaust. We followed them into Bridgewater to the Ford Dealership there and left their car to be repaired. Then we all travelled to North Petherton in our car to start today's walk to Catcott.

Field paths *(poor footpaths here)* to the outskirts of Bridgewater, passing industrial units, along neglected paths with rubbish scattered here and there: we didn't see the best of Bridgewater here. We crossed the canal via a bridge next to a railway and made our way toward one of the scarce footbridges over the very busy M5 motorway. With great relief we left Bridgewater behind us and eventually were out of earshot of the traffic on the motorway. After crossing the motorway we were on the Somerset Levels, field drains alongside us, with some pretty wild flowers, bulrushes, pink campion and teasels.

Chedzoy Church (lunch stop)

Wild flowers and bulrushes alongside the lane

King's Sedgemoor Drain

Part lane walking and some fields, and on better paths now, we came to the village of Chedzoy – Sedgemoor country – site of the Battle of Sedgemoor in the Civil War. We had a 'late' picnic lunch in the churchyard at Chedzoy.

Some lane walking from here, then footpaths again, over a very flat landscape until we reached the Polden Hills – not high, but gave some scenic interest. Up and over this hill, crossing the Roman Road (A39), and down the other side: and now we had a view of the Mendip Hills. Field edge paths to the village of Edington and on to Catcott, from where we had a taxi back to Bridgewater (to retrieve Bob's car which had to undergo a repair). On then to collect our car from North Petherton and return to site.

Day 19 **Thursday 28th July 2011** **Catcott to Draycott** **14.0 miles**

From Catcott across fields to Shapwick Heath along a wooded track: drainage ditches, ponds and marshland, and grazing fields either side (some hayfield and some cattle) for quite a few miles until we reached the road to Westhay. Kept on along roads with a view of Glastonbury Tor in the distance: marshland drains evident and much peat – tractor loads frequently passing us around here.

By Avalon Marshes Visitor Centre still road walking and passing American Longhorn Cattle grazing the scrubland. Then another track – a drovers road – straight for a good couple of miles or so, then lanes.

On to the country town / village of Wedmore where we had a coffee stop. This was an 'upmarket' and well-off village with many ladies' fashion shops, boutiques and craft shops, gifts and accessories.

Evidently a destination for 'ladies who lunch': we felt quite out of place in our walking gear and rucksacks.

Out of Wedmore across a few fields and heading uphill to cross the inevitable golf course *(for the husbands of the 'ladies who lunch'?)*. Just missed a flying golf ball here so found a 'safe spot', in front of some trees and with a good view, for our picnic lunch.

Sheep enjoying the view

Lunch stop after Wedmore village

A mix of road and lanes and paths until we reached Nyland Hill, which we decided we *had* to climb: it being a notable landmark amongst the otherwise flat countryside.

Nyland Hill

There were good views to Cheddar, Brent Knoll (alongside the M5 motorway), the Quantock Hills (behind us now), Glastonbury Tor and the Mendip Hills (tomorrow's walk).

The top of Nyland Hill

View from Nyland Hill across to the Mendip Hills

Only a short walk from here to site, and as it was a beautiful day we decided to have our evening meal together, sitting outside in the late afternoon sun.

Day 20 **Friday 29th July 2011** **Draycott to Paulton** **17.8 miles**

Uphill from Draycott onto the Mendip Hills, with views over the Somerset Levels, albeit rather grey and misty today in the drizzly rain. Once up on the top of the hills we took a downward track past woodland and out again into fields, then headed uphill once more over the hills of Cheddar Gorge: crossing the road at the top of the Gorge to enter Black Rock Nature Reserve on a woodland track which opened out to a valley with limestone outcrops, similar to Cavedale in the Peak District. We then were in Velvet Bottom Nature Reserve: aptly named because of the short velvety green grass on the flat sections of each level of past mining activity around here.

Velvet Bottom

This went on for quite a way, each level higher than the previous one. We eventually reached the top and then had some lanes to walk for a while before crossing meadows overlooking the village of Compton Martin. We decided this was a good spot for our picnic lunch.

Lunch stop at Compton Martin

On through fields to another village where we had a cup of tea at the pub. *(On requesting tea, Lynne got the distinct impression that this particular pub didn't often serve this modest type of beverage!)* From here we saw our first road signpost to Bath. We headed uphill out of the village and then across several freshly cut hay fields and a long wild flower meadow overlooking Cameley Meadows and other small villages beyond.

Along by a stream for several fields and eventually through woodland crossing the stream and heading uphill on the other side. A very poor path along the edge of a sweetcorn crop forced us to take a path along the old railway until our turn off path to Paulton where the car was parked.

Day 21 **Saturday 30th July 2011** **Paulton to Bath** **18.7 miles**

Our last walking day, for this section, started with rainfall while we had breakfast – although the weather forecast was predicting sunshine today! To be fair, by the time we'd driven to Paulton and parked Bob's car it was dry, although still overcast. We set off through Paulton and then alongside 'Jenny's Path': a route alongside an old canal that served the coal mines in the 1800s. To begin with we were passing gypsy caravans and tents in fields nearby, but soon we were further away from the town and heading to Camerton – an old coal mining town: like Paulton. There was a coal mining trail here that we started along by mistake: on a high embankment that had been used for a railway. This was interesting but we quickly realised that this wasn't our route and retraced our steps to once again follow the route of the old canal. For much of the way we followed the River Cam, and then Cam Brook through very pretty countryside, arable fields and hills and 'very English Countryside' views, with mature trees, woodland, and pasture land.

Cam Brook

Passing through the village of Coombe Hay we came across The Wheat Sheaf Pub / Restaurant, beautifully situated and a lovely old building, but very contemporary in its décor. Clearly 'the place to go', locally. As we were just nearing the 300 mile point in our walk it seemed an excellent plan to celebrate this and have a drink – it had now become the hot sunny day that was forecast and we were all quite warm! We had our photo taken together, by a couple who had earlier asked us the way to the pub as we'd walked through this village.

300 miles – Wheat Sheaf Pub, Coombe Hay

We discussed the route. Yesterday we had thought to take the shorter route into Bath today, rather than the previously planned circuit round the southern side of Bath and into the city from the east side, but as we were making good time and the weather was good we reverted to our original plan, so, shortly after leaving the pub we went across fields following a disused canal for a while, the walk being along the old tow-path, and we were heading for the Kennet and Avon Canal and Dundas Aqueduct.

Disused canal seen clearly here

Through fields, still on the old tow path and with good views and interesting countryside, we stopped for lunch along here. Later in the afternoon we reached the Dundas Aqueduct over the River Cam and the railway, and were now alongside the Kennet and Avon Canal *(still very much in use – we passed several canal boats here)* and walking at a very brisk pace *(set by Bob and Andy)*.

Dundas Aqueduct

We stopped at a canal bridge for a short break before going up and over Cleeveton Down, past Bath University and the golf course. We passed a pony riding event and then were, eventually, rewarded with views of Bath from the 'Sham Castle'. However, there was still quite a bit of walking to do. Heading downhill into the city, and crossing the river with a view of Poultney Bridge, we reached Bath Abbey at 5.30 pm. We took the necessary photos of each other, and had an even more necessary ice-cream, before walking to the bus station and catching a bus back to Paulton.

The City of Bath ahead

Poultney Bridge, Bath

Andy, Meg and Zak reach Bath Abbey

We'd walked 18.7 miles today, giving us a walk total for this section of 310 miles.

This evening, back at site, we celebrated by having a meal at 'The Gardener's Arms' in Cheddar. A very good meal in pleasant and friendly surroundings. An excellent end to our our first three weeks of 'LeJog'.

Day 22 **Saturday 15th October 2011** **Bath Abbey to Tormarton** **16.7 miles**

We arrived at North Nibley yesterday to stay at North Nibley Farm. The site is up in the orchard with panoramic views towards the Severn Estuary. A good sunset meant that we could also see the River Severn and the hills beyond – across into the Forest of Dean.

This morning we drove to Tormarton, leaving at 8.45 am, and parked our car. We had booked a taxi from the pub 'Major's Retreat', to take us from there to Bath Abbey to start the day's walk. It had the promise of a lovely sunny day. We first had a look around the Abbey: lovely vaulted light stone roof and a large high stained glass window at the altar end and opposite. The other windows were clear glass and this had the effect of a lovely 'light' space. The Abbey Organ was impressive, as was the illuminated manuscript in the 'Book of Remembrance': commemorating those who had been killed in the two World Wars.

Book of Remembrance
WW1 and WW2

It just chanced that we were there to see a most beautiful and inspiring display of 25 Diptychs: one half of each diptych was a painting and the partner to each painting was a needlework picture of the same subject. Depicting the Life of Christ, these Diptychs were the craftsmanship of Sue Symons. Completed in one year, 2006-2007, these were the result of 30,000 hours of work.

Having thoroughly enjoyed our brief look in the Cathedral we then took a photograph of the four of us outside the Abbey before we started our second section of LeJog. (*No dog to join us this time: Zak died after a short illness in August this year*).

We started the Cotswold Way going out of Bath through Victoria Park, where there was a noisy outcry from Magpies and two Jays, fighting overhead. Through the park the path was, of course, uphill, as all roads out of Bath are!!

Lynne, Bob, Andy and Meg outside Bath Abbey

From there up and down to Penn Hill and through Weston. Then on towards the Racecourse and Lansdown Hill, the site of a major battle in the Civil War in 1643. A little further on from there we had our lunch stop. Impressive views all around so far, and glorious sunshine.

On to Cold Ashton where there was a magnificent Manor House and Entrance Gate, and then to Pennsylvania: a chance for a cup of coffee (purchased at the nearby garage) which we took with us, finding a suitable spot to sit and enjoy this, before continuing our walk which took us to Dyrham village and Dyrham Park and House *(National Trust)*. The route took us around the perimeter wall of the park and then out on to farmland, passing an area of 'strip lynchets' (medieval farming) on the way.

Strip Lynchets near Dyrham Park

Hot air balloon near Tormarton

We then came towards the busy M4 motorway, and we were parallel with the motorway for the mile or so on the path towards Tormarton, finally crossing it on a bridge not far from Tormarton Village and we were soon back at the car.

There were several hot air balloons up today: a perfect day for it.

After driving back to site we went down to the Black Horse Inn for an evening meal, which made a good end to a lovely first day of walking the Cotswold Way as part of our long walk to John O'Groats.

Day 23   **Sunday 16th October 2011**   **Tormarton to North Nibley**   **19.0 miles**

Drove to Tormarton and left Bob's car there, then it was a very pleasant walk across Doddington Park – rolling parkland for several miles. From there to Old Sodbury and up to the church where on a clear day could be seen the two Severn Bridge Crossings. The early morning cloud was just lifting and so we couldn't yet see that far away. We had a look in the church: as a parishioner was just opening up in time for the morning service, and she was very helpful. Leaving the church we then walked up to Sodbury Hill Fort, with great views to Chipping Sodbury Church and town, the rolling English countryside looking fantastic in the morning autumn sunshine.

Up and over the fort which was quite extensive. From the fort we took the path down toward Little Sodbury, past St Adeline's Church and on to Horton, where there was a grand house and a circular building specially for Swallows and Owls. From the house we went on past the village of Horton, across the valley, and Horton Church.

A wide path along field edges, with good views to our left took us to the village of Hawkesbury Upton, the skylarks singing to us as we approached the pub 'The Monument': where we had cups of hot chocolate to keep us going until lunchtime.

Along the road for a very short while to a monument where we turned right down a farm track to Lower Kilcott.

The Monument

Kilcott Valley

Down the road to Kilcott Mill and along this very pretty valley for several miles, stopping in a field in the sunshine, and in the shelter of the valley, to have our lunch. At the end of the valley we came out to Alderley passing a folly at Winner Hill. A sunken lane down to the stream and then field paths to Wortley. Another sunken lane going up to Wortley Hill, rising very steeply for quite a while. Round to a viewpoint where there were great views of the two Severn Bridges, and over to Wales, the Forest of Dean, the Brecon Beacons, and the Black Mountains in the far distance.

Along the hill to a lane which went steeply down, and then through woodland and on further to a stream, which we followed into Wotton-under-Edge. Children, with their fishing nets, playing in the stream along here. We followed the path by the stream until we came into the town by the church where we had our 'flapjack' stop. The path then took us through the town, passing a courtyard of almshouses and a chapel, and then we were out along the road towards North Nibley.

Shortly after leaving the town we had our final steep *'up'* through woodland back on to the hilltop, following a field edge with woodland on our left. We followed this for about two miles until we reached Brackenbury Ditches *(hill fort)* and then a little later on came out of the trees into the open at Nibley Knoll where the views to the Severn were even better, and the sun was just starting to go down. We could now see the Tyndale Monument: across the grassland and up on the hill. Andy and Bob decided to go to the top of the Monument, as it was open. Lynne and I, being the more sensible pair, decided to stay at the bottom (as we had very good views to look at there anyway) and watched the menfolk as they emerged at the top. It was a steep descent to the village of North Nibley, and then we just had to follow the lane through the village to the site. Andy and Bob went off to retrieve Bob's car back while Lynne and I cooked dinner.

Tyndale Monument, North Nibley

Day 24   Monday 17th October 2011   North Nibley to Randwick Church   16 miles

Andy and Bob took our car to Randwick Church, coming back to site again in Bob's car, while Lynne and I made the packed lunches. We left site to walk to Randwick at 9.10 am and started off across fields away from North Nibley and towards Stinchcombe Hill.

We had quite a climb up through woodland on a sunken path covered in autumn leaves, before contouring round the side of the hillside and up to Stinchcombe Hill where the Cotswold Way did a convoluted circuit round this hilltop, around the golf course, and around the perimeter of the hill with stunning views out on all sides

We then took a very steep woodland path down to the town of Dursley, where we stopped at a bakery for hot chocolate and bacon rolls (for the lads) and Belgian Buns (for the ladies).

It was as well that we did, as the next section was a *very steep 'up'* and along the ridge of Cam Long Down, from where there were views both sides into the steep valleys below: views to the Malverns on one side and views back to the Tyndale Monument and Stinchcombe Hill, that we'd now left behind.

Leaving North Nibley, heading for Stinchcombe

Looking back to Stinchcombe Hill with the Tyndale Monument still in sight

Coming down from Cam Long Down was on a steep grassy slope down to Hodgecombe Farm, and then we were climbing very steeply up again through woods to a road.

This was a very long steep section and we were thankful for the seat at the top to have a rest and admire the views before carrying on to Coaley Peak where the views were magnificent at the grassy top. There was a picnic area and we sat and had our lunch: in a sheltered spot out of the freshening breeze, at one of the picnic tables.

Coaley Peak

We then walked across the grassland past Nymphfield Barrow and then through more woodland, Buckshot Wood, Stanley Wood and Penn Wood to the village of Middleyard.

On to Kings Stanley and Stanley Hill before crossing a disused canal (but still with water in it) and the Oxford to Worcester Railway line, past Wycliffe School and then up several grassy fields to reach woodland, where we turned off the Cotswold Way steeply downhill to Randwick Church and our waiting car.

Stunning view from Coaley Peak

Day 25   Tuesday 18th October 2011   Randwick Church to Cooper's Hill   11.4 miles

We awoke, after a very stormy, blustery night, to sunshine and clear blue skies and, although colder than previously, it was good walking weather. We took the cars to the start and finish of today's walk and were walking by 9.30 am. Up from Randwick Church, our legs now recovered from yesterday's ups and downs, we managed this section better than anticipated and we were soon on the higher ground to rejoin the Cotswold Way at yesterday's finishing point.

Through Randwick Wood and past some ancient burial mounds *(not just lumps and bumps)* on to Standish Wood, where we emerged from the woods out onto open ground and a viewpoint.

Randwick Wood

Then round the edge of woodland and out to Bunkers Bank and up to Haresfield Beacon.

The path up to Haresfield Beacon

After this we were into more woodland until we reached disused quarries *(drink stop)* where there were now many silver birch trees. Across the valley was Painswick Church, our next destination.

View to Painswick village and church

55 miles from Bath, 45 miles to go on the Cotswold Way

Down the hill from the old quarry we came across a Cotswold Way marker stone showing that we were 55 miles from Bath and 45 miles away from Chipping Campden: so well over half way now. On and up again into Painswick, where we stopped for a 'hot chocolate' in a quaint and attractive delicatessen. It was very good hot chocolate, and we could sit down in the warm to have it.

Our cafe stop in Painswick

From Painswick we made our way to Painswick Common and passing a quarry for *Painswick Stone* we then were out into the open on the area of the hill fort, where we stopped to have our lunch.

Hill fort after Painswick Common

Just 2.5 miles to go now and much of this was through woodland until we reached Cooper's Hill and Brockworth Hill (the *scene of many a 'cheese rolling' down a very steep incline – and according to one local, also the scene of many a race 'up the incline'.)*

Back to site at North Nibley and a 'pack up and move' to Greet, near Winchcombe, for the next stages of the walk.

Day 26   Wednesday 19th October 2011   Cooper's Hill to Ham Hill   16 miles

Leaving Bob's car just past Ham Hill, we then drove to Cooper's Hill to start today's walk.

We started walking through woodland for quite some distance, across Cooper's Hill, Buckholt Wood and Witcombe Wood, and we were 'motoring' along at 3.4 mph.

Beech woodland at Coopers Hill

Eventually we came out into the open and into sunshine on Birdlip Hill: with a view of Crickley Hill; our first objective.

Before that we had to reach 'The Peak' and a viewpoint at 'Barrow Wake'. We then came out on the very busy A417 leading to the junction with the A436 at The Air Balloon pub. Here we stopped for a very good 'hot chocolate', complete with amaretto biscuits, after which we had to cross the very busy road junction *(not easy)*.

On grassland and then out onto Crickley Hill where there were good views to both Gloucester and Cheltenham. Another bright but cold day today with perfect visibility. A little road walking later took us past The National Star College, and then we were on a good path by fields heading uphill for a while to Leckhampton Hill and The Devil's Chimney.

View across to Gloucester

The Devil's Chimney

There was some rain coming in at this point and for the first time this holiday out came the waterproofs, but not for too long, and we soon found a place just past the trig point, at the tumulus, in a sheltered spot out of the wind for our lunch stop.

Magnificent views as we walked upon Charlton Kings Common

From there it was hillwalking along to Charlton Kings Common, which was very steep sided, and then coming down from that we made our way to the road crossing at Seven Springs.

Heading uphill on a footpath parallel to the A436 we were climbing steadily to Wistley Grove Wood and Wistley Hill, then on through Lineover Wood and down to the cross the A40. Another climb up to Dowdeswell Reservoir and Wood, continually climbing until we came out by Colgate Farm.

After that, a more gentle wide path along the top of Ham Hill, until we joined the lane which took us back to the car, just beyond Ham Hill.

Approaching our waiting car at Ham Hill

Back to collect our car and then a 'food shop and fuel stop' before coming back to site.

Day 27   Thursday 20th October 2011   Ham Hill to Stanway   15.8 miles

It was a cold frosty start this morning with ice on the windscreen to be scraped before we could drive, and then park, just beyond Ham Hill. Walking at first to Prestbury Hill, which is a nature reserve, we had bright sunshine, but frost on the ground in the shade.

We heard birdsong all around us as we walked: robins, skylarks, warblers and blackbirds. With excellent views across Prestbury Hill and on up to Cleeve Hill, where there were more grand vistas, this was an excellent start to the day.

View from Prestbury Hill

Walking down Cleeve Hill

The eastern side of Cleeve Hill

Warmer today in the sunshine and with less breeze than yesterday. We saw many dog walkers, and golfers, on Cleeve Hill – a popular spot. Our route took us round the east of Cleeve Hill and then down across meadows to reach 'Belas Knapp' Long Barrow.

Meg, at the sign to Belas Knapp

From there a revised Cotswold Way Route took us down through pasture land, mainly grazed by horses, and then briefly along the River Isbourne, approaching Winchcombe uphill by the castle road, bringing us out opposite the church.

Once in Winchcombe we sat on a seat by the church, facing the main street through the town, to eat our lunch. We then walked through the town and stopped for a hot drink at a tea room run by a Japanese family. *(Awards had been won for their tea shop).*

View towards Studely Castle, before Winchcombe

Out of Winchcombe over the river bridge: where there used to be a ford and a footbridge, and then a right turn uphill and gentle walking to Hailes Abbey.

'Raised' Barn before Stanway

Stanway Mill

Now the final climb of the day up to a monument: at first going through woodland and then across sheep pasture land, rising steeply, to reach the monument *(flapjack stop!)*. Across another field to join a track past a 'raised barn' to a road, and, finally, across more fields to Stanway Mill and Tithe Barn and on to Bob's car. Collected our car, then had fish and chips from Winchcombe.

Day 28 **Friday 21st October 2011** **Stanway to Chipping Campden** **12.3 miles**

From Stanway across fields to Stanton: a very attractive village with cottages and houses in Cotswold stone.

Leaving Stanway

A cottage in Stanton

Then uphill for a while before the way levelled out across pastureland Heading down on a wide track we had Broadway village in our sights. Across grassy fields to Broadway church: a very pastoral scene with sheep grazing amidst the autumnal setting.

Approaching Broadway Church

Andy and Bob at Broadway Tower

Once in picturesque Broadway we had coffee and cakes to give us the strength to walk up Broadway Hill to Broadway Tower. After a steep, but worthwhile, climb we reached the Tower and, after admiring the views from the top, continued on our way across fields and woodland, with developing autumn colours, to Saintbury Picnic area where we ate our lunch.

From here we walked across arable fields and then, finally, on a wide grassy path to Dover's Hill. Along Dover's Hill: with more views, and then we were on a path along field edges to the outskirts of Chipping Campden: the beautiful Cotswold stone buildings looking at their best in the sunshine. We arrived in the centre of Chipping Campden at 3.15 pm and took the required end of walk photos.

Our first view of Chipping Campden

The four of us at the end of the Cotswold Way in Chipping Campden

We noted where the Heart of England Way started: in preparation for next year's walking, and made our way to the Barton Tea Rooms for a cup of tea / hot chocolate to celebrate finishing the Cotswold Way. Andy nobly offered to walk back to Dover's Hill and collect our car, while we finished our tea, and we met him just 20 minutes later in the main street. Drove back to Stanway, to Bob's car, and made our way back to site.

Meal at the Royal Oak booked for 7 pm tonight to celebrate that we've now walked 400 miles since Land's End. We shall continue our walk in July 2012: starting along the Heart of England Way as part of our route next year to Malham Tarn in Yorkshire.

Day 29   Saturday 14th July 2012   Chipping Campden to Stratford-upon-Avon   16.2 miles

Starting off walking from Chipping Campden Market Place, where we finished the Cotswold Way last year, we then took the Heart of England Way past the school and the church.

Across very wet grassy fields to Mickleton Hills Farm. Then some lane walking before reaching a more broken-surfaced lane to a boundary stone seat *(2012)*. From here 'ridge and furrow' fields: or rather, in this wet summer, 'ridge and lakes', to reach Hidcote Manor, where we stopped at the National Trust cafe for tea and cakes – there were some particularly cheeky chaffinches here who rather liked the look of Lynne's cake, swooping down over the table to try and get a crumb or two!

From Hidcote it was very hard going because of the *very wet and muddy* arable fields, and uphill walking was made very difficult as we made our way through barley and then tall broad bean plants: the waterlogged fields and running water resulting in very muddy boots and legs. Several fields later we reached Upper Quinton – where Bob narrowly avoided a drenching as a passing car made its way through the flooded road – and then on to Lower Quinton and more field walking to the old railway at Long Marston station.

We had lunch here: and made an attempt to clean muddy over-trousers, before setting off heading northwards to Stratford-upon-Avon on four miles of considerably firmer and drier path along the old railway, and we made good progress.

Stopping only to partake of refreshments from a railway carriage cafe at Milcote crossing, we made our way into the town via the riverside path.

The River Avon here was very high and out over its banks – no rowing boats or river boats today! The riverside bench seats were surrounded by water, and Andy climbed onto one of these to have a photo taken.

Once at the river bridge we continued our walk, passing the Royal Shakespeare Company Theatre on the way to our waiting car.

Day 30   Sunday 15th July 2012   Stratford-upon-Avon to Shrewley   14.6 miles

From Greenway Car Park we walked along the river into Stratford-upon-Avon – a drier day today but the River Avon was even higher than yesterday. Once in the town we looked at the 'tourist spots': Shakespeare's birthplace etc., before finding the start of the Stratford-upon-Avon canal, which we followed northwards, passing Wilmcott flight of locks and various small interestingly designed bridges over the canal. Narrow boats, walkers and joggers we passed as we made good headway with good walking conditions, despite the occasional 'very muddy' sections of towpath.

An abundance of wild flowers and families of ducklings made for interesting walking. At around 11 am we came off the tow-path and headed to Mary Arden's House where we enjoyed a coffee stop, while watching sheep-shearing 'Tudor' style!

Back to the canal and heading north again, we walked beside the Edstone Aqueduct – longest in England. On to Wooton Wawen Aqueduct and Wooton Wawen Locks where we had lunch, entertained by a family of ducklings being fed by a narrow boat owner – they were clearly used to doing that!! On further to the smallest of the three aqueducts along this canal, and eventually to Lowsonford Lock, where we left the canal to go across fields in the direction of Shrewley.

Passing a small chapel, with a seat, we stopped to have 'flapjacks' before continuing over, and up, fields to Shrewley. We saw a deer at the far side of the field and Lynne and I were so engrossed in looking at the deer we failed to spot the *bull* amongst the cows until we reached the gate at the far side. Probably just as well – it saved our heart-rates rising! A short walk from there, up quite wet fields, to the road to our site at Pitts Farm. Weather *dry all day* today!!

Day 31   Monday July 16th 2012   Pitts Farm, near Shrewley, to Meriden   14.2 miles

We walked from site into Shrewley and took a footpath through a tunnel down to the canal: which was in another tunnel below. We followed the canal for just over two miles and then we took the lane to Rowington. From Rowington we went across fields – through a cow field, and then on an extremely overgrown path, narrow with brambles, nettles and thistles, and very muddy underfoot. This was the story of the day: *sodden fields and quantities of standing water along the route.* It rained until about 2 pm, when we had lunch. We took field paths and some woodland paths towards Baddesley Clinton, *(National Trust)* but it was too early to stop there for coffee as it didn't open until 11am.

On over more fields, wet and muddy, through barley, wheat and rape and the occasional cow field: some very lovely calves in one, and then we found a 'trendy' pub open in Chadwick End, Baddesley Clinton, where we sat outside under cover to have our hot chocolate, which came complete with marshmallows and a twisty doughnut, and was most welcome.

From there along the road a little way before more fields – all very wet on the ground, the tall crops and grass making everything wet, along with the rain coming down from above to add to the overall wetness. One field was particularly, and exceptionally, hard-going – uphill on slippery mud through a tall sweetcorn crop. Also difficult, another wheat field with an 'impromptu' lake at the start. Some of the barley looked ready to harvest: it was very golden in colour, but unless we get some dry weather for a while the farmers will all be having a very difficult harvest this year.

When the rain ceased early afternoon we had difficulty finding somewhere to stop and have our sandwiches as everywhere was so wet. Eventually we ended up on a grassy verge, sitting on our respective 'orange survival bags' at the side of the road. After lunch we crossed more fields to Berkwell: very attractive and unusual church. The village too was very pretty, complete with a village 'well' and 'stocks'. On from there: after looking inside the church, which had a 'west gallery' and sloping floor in the nave – and which, after all was a *dry* place to go, so who can blame us for that – we went on through fields of wheat, barley and rapeseed to reach the 'Heart of England' – the village of Meriden, where the car was.

After returning to site and taking off our *very wet clothes*, reviving with a cup of tea and a 'wash and change' into dry clothes, we went to the local restaurant for a very 'posh' meal – we think we deserve it after a very wet, soggy day! Hoping it will be drier tomorrow, although it is still raining as I write this. It will take several days of hot sunny weather to dry up the fields.

Day 32 **Tuesday 17th July 2012** **Meriden to Hurley** **13.7miles**

We started today at Meriden Churchyard, where I took a photo of the four of us at the 'Heart of England'.

Downhill from the church through cow fields: much better underfoot than yesterday as the grass was dry and the ground firmer here at least. Crossed the old A45 then on a lane to a caravan park after which we went through more fields and some woodland, still on the Heart of England Way. All was going well until we crossed the M6: with views to Birmingham; and reached the cow fields of the next farm.

There was no way of walking across the fields without getting extremely, and disgustingly, muddy, and it was a very precarious event – danger of landing in several inches of mud, or not being able to move at all: with both feet sinking deeper into the mire being a real possibility. With very muddy trousers and boots, and making exceptionally slow progress, we eventually made it across.

In complete contrast, a mile or so further on we were in a beautiful wild flower meadow with a view across rolling English countryside. However, there was no room for complacency

here as just after that was a *huge* field of rapeseed, admittedly with a path through it, but it was very sticky and uneven underfoot: horseflies added to the delights of this section, succeeding in annoying us and resulting in a few bites all round.

Then mainly arable fields, predominantly wheat, with a *good* wide path through, and later, some woodland before we reached our lunch stop at Shustoke Reservoir. We had a couple of 'tough-going' fields of wheat, as it was very wet and slippery uphill through these: one of which, again, was vast, to then reach a long and muddy track, dark with trees, alongside the railway – more insect bites. The pub we hoped for at Whiteacre failed to materialise and so we kept on until we reached Hurley – all quite tired on the last mile or so after the wheat field, but we made it.

I was *very* pleased to take boots off (despite boots being unpleasantly muddy) and to sit down in the car for the journey back to site.

Day 33   Thursday 19th July 2012   Hurley to Bucks Head Farm   12 miles
(Old Watling Street) near Weeford.

We walked from Hurley on field paths through wheat, and then down to the river Tame, passing a grand house: newly renovated with what looked like old castle walls, but nothing marked on the map. A raised footpath took us to the river bridge. We then crossed river meadows to the lakes of Kingsbury Water Park. Some *'Monet-like'* water lilies flowering here.

Through the park a little way, and passing the Camping and Caravanning Club Site, we reached the Birmingham and Fazeley Canal where we progressed at a great rate – 4.6 mph at one point – along a good towpath.

We came off the towpath at a canal bridge, to cross a main road, before heading in the direction of the village of Drayton Bassett – burial place of Sir Robert Peel who founded the Police Force *(Peelers)*.

From here we had some lane walking for a while, passing some nicely converted barns at Binley Barns – an impressive farmhouse here too. On past Hints Farm, where there was a sign 'Jam and Marmalade for sale': but there was no-one in when Bob and Lynne knocked at the door to buy.

From Hints Farm, at first going across farmland and then some more hilly grassland: sheep grazing, we reached our lunch stop on Gorsey Hill. After lunch we headed down through a pretty grassy valley, also with sheep, and then through fields to the old A5 Watling Street Roman Road, and our waiting car.

| Day 34 | Friday 20th July 2012 | Bucks Head Farm to Pipe Hill Wood | 7.88 miles |

(beyond Lichfield)

An easier day's walking planned today so that we could enjoy exploring Lichfield on our way through.

We set off through Bucks Head farm yard on a wide track at first, then on a narrow downhill track where *tall* and *wet* grasses and wild flowers resulted in *wet trouser legs* for a while. From a grassy track later, across farmland, we had our first sighting of the three spires of Lichfield Cathedral.

We were on a good track now, passing a traditional old farm, with lovely wild flowers in the surrounding countryside. Later on, walking between evenly spaced young trees, we had ever closer views of Lichfield. We were now on the outskirts of the city and walking through housing estates, passing a short section of the Lichfield Canal undergoing restoration. Still on the Heart of England Way, and amongst houses: way-marks set into the pavements keeping us right on our route, we continued uphill and out onto Borrow Cop Hill, where there was a red sandstone building housing a seat. From here was a good view to the Cathedral *(sadly spoiled by a 1960s school building ahead of us: a soul-less building with nothing to commend it at all, making us wonder what the city planners were thinking of)*. Bob tried to get a good photo of the Cathedral by standing on top of the seat, and thereby not getting the offending building in the picture at all!

On through more houses: very reminiscent of our walk down to Bath Abbey last summer, and into a shopping centre precinct. Indulged in hot chocolate / posh coffee – very welcome, before exploring the city. We made our way to the Cathedral, which was very impressive, and on the way passed The Tudor Inn. As we've now walked 500 miles since Land's End we decided it was time for a celebratory meal and so booked a table at the aforesaid Inn, for lunch. Andy and I visited the birthplace of Samuel Johnson who compiled the first English Dictionary: published in 1755; commissioned in 1746.

After a very good lunch, we couldn't leave Lichfield without another visit to the Cathedral, after which we continued on our way out of the city through a park and then into countryside, down Abnall's Lane to Pipe Hill Wood, and the waiting car.

Day 35   Saturday 21st July 2012   Lichfield (Pipe Hill Wood) to Rugeley   12.9 miles

We carried on following the Heart of England Way and were soon on a lane through Cannock Chase, passing bracken-covered woodland to our left and houses on the right, until we reached Gentleshaw, where the gateway to the parish church was bedecked in a garland of flowers for a wedding: very attractive.

From there were grand houses as we walked uphill to a pub: where we stopped for hot chocolate and the very chatty landlady joined us as we sat enjoying our mid-morning drink. On from here we passed a 2000 year old castle mound before entering into woodland, passing the Camping and Caravanning Club Cannock Chase Site, and then onto forestry tracks, where we enjoyed watching mountain bikers at Stiles Cop tearing downhill and over jumps.

A little further on, towards Birches Wood, teenagers were having a lot of fun on the zip-wires and high tree climbs at a 'Go-Ape' Centre. Once at the Birches Wood Forest Centre we sat at a secluded picnic table for our picnic lunch – very civilised – before heading up and out of 'The Chase'.

As we were leaving we saw the start of a race: there were many runners.

Nearby was this wooden sculpture of a walking boot, which we thought appropriate for us!

Leaving Cannock Chase we went through fields before climbing up to Etchinghill, with its rocky outcrop at the top.

Down to the outskirts of Rugely: we skirted around the town for a while to reach the Trent and Mersey Canal which we followed across Brindleys Aqueduct into the town of Rugeley.

A short walk from here back to site and a welcome cup of tea and some tea-bread from Bob and Lynne.

A lovely sunny day today – we sat outside for our evening meal – Lynne made a fruit crumble for pudding – all very nice and relaxing.

Day 36 **Sunday 22nd July 2012** **Rugeley to Uttoxeter** **13.2 miles**

Walking from site we crossed freshly cut hay fields and hay meadows to the village of Stockwell Heath, which was pretty, having a village pond complete with yellow water-lilies.

Gradually going uphill from here, still through fields, we had a view of the Rugeley Power Station in the distance behind us, and ahead of us the Blithfield Reservoir. We left the reservoir at the dam and headed away for a short while on a track before turning to walk parallel to the dam. We then crossed a bridge over a stream before heading uphill again, away from the reservoir, across fields to the village of Abbots Bromley.

This was an attractive village with a butter market, four pubs (sadly, none of which were open yet) and a village green. Many black and white half timbered houses here.

As the pubs weren't open we sat on a seat on the green to have a mid-morning drink and flapjack stop. Nearby, we read of the tradition of the Abbots Bromley Horn Dance.

Hot and sunny by now, with blue sky overhead for most of the day.

Leaving Abbots Bromley behind us we walked alongside some rape fields, through long grass, which today thankfully was dry in the sunny weather: or we would have got very wet again!

Just before Baggot Wood we turned right, to cross fields on a track – still wet in places from the recent rain – then down past a farm and recently modernised barn conversions and on to a lane. Stopped for lunch at the side of the lane – we couldn't find a better spot.

After lunch and still following the Staffordshire Way, we encountered a really-badly-kept and very muddy farm. Picking our way through the muck on the farm drive was bad, but the section through the gate was even worse, with a very sticky, muddy and mucky cow field to follow.

We were all pleased to leave this particular farm behind us, and continued along more hay fields to reach Uttoxeter. Back to the car and a hunt for ice-creams before heading back to site.

Quite a difficult day with *many* stiles, which were all high and very narrow: often between overgrown hedges; and some narrow paths through long grasses. However, the Peak District is in view with the prospect of much better walking, and the weather is dry!

Day 37   **Monday 23rd July 2012**   **Uttoxeter to Blore (near Dovedale)**   **13.7 miles**

We left Uttoxeter across water meadows, then crossed the A50 to Dove Bridge, to go through a muddy field – cows again – and then uphill behind Sidford Wood. It was really warm and the horseflies were about making it a bit unpleasant for us, along with the nettles, brambles and thistles. However we eventually emerged onto a track past nicely kept green grass to a corporate business shooting venue.

After this we were on quite a good double width track for a while, then across fields to the village of Rocester – and the old Arkwright Mill: now a JCB Academy. Along from here were some new houses built in a Victorian style which suited their surroundings. A little further on we were able to get a cup of coffee from the village shop, to take away, and we had this sat on the village seat.

Suitably refreshed, we left Rocester heading up to Barrow Hill where we were pleased to get a view of rolling countryside around us. Grazing sheep in short (dry!) grass – *it doesn't take a lot to make us happy*, as this was the promise of excellent walking country ahead!

Crossed a hayfield to the River Dove, which we followed on a wide path, then grassy track – all very pleasant, with geese and goslings enjoying the river. Mostly reasonable paths to the river bridge at Lower Ellastone. Here the river went eastward for a while: we carried on in a more northerly direction across fields, with squeeze-stiles in the dry-stone walls: rather a feature of the Peak District, that prove challenging when you're not tall and have a rucksack on your back. However, this always supplies a ready source of amusement to my fellow walkers. Eventually crossing the Ashbourne Road we were on a narrow lane heading to Blore. Steadily climbing much of the way today until just before Blore Village where the view opened up – Dove Dale and Thorpe Cloud ahead of us. Views to the Peak District and our way ahead.

Different wild flowers today: a clump of blue 'daisy-like' flowers we found were chicory and there was also a lovely patch of harebells on the hillside.

Looking forward to some good walking ahead of us now – that will make us forget the mud and very wet fields we've encountered in the last week or so. This evening we had a meal at 'The Yorkshireman': a few hundred yards from site. We then paid our site fees and will move site tomorrow: which will mean a day off from walking.

Day 38   **Wednesday 25th July 2012**   **Blore to Hartington**   **10.2 miles**

From Blore to Coldwall Farm we took a track past the farm to Coldwall Bridge, over the River Dove, and came back into Derbyshire to take the path past Thorpe Cloud heading for the stepping stones at Dovedale. Due to all the recent heavy rain two of the stepping stones were out of place, which meant there weren't the usual queues of people waiting to get across at this popular tourist spot.

We walked up Dove Dale, all very pretty and excellent walking as we'd known. So many photo opportunities now. From Dove Dale we progressed into Mill Dale, where we had a stop for hot chocolate and cake, happily watching the ducks as we sat by the river. Then along the road next to the river for a while, passing some cottages and then coming back to the river, still in Mill Dale and onto Ashbourne Meadows: the steep sided valleys here are beautiful. We carried on along the Dove into Beresford Dale – different again with its weirs and rippling water – all very peaceful.

We had our lunch sat next to the river in a shady spot a few miles short of Hartington. Saw a heron flying along the river – silent wings above us – and also two dippers on the far bank.

At the end of Beresford Dale we came out onto river meadows, very green and pleasant, before taking a track up and over and then down into the very picturesque village of Hartington. We enjoyed a cup of tea at a cafe before deliberating which cheeses to purchase from the selection in Hartington Cheese Factory Shop.

An excellent walk today, with great scenery and blessed with good weather to make it perfect. So *no muddy boots today* – so appreciative are we of this.

| Day 39 | Thursday 26th July 2012 | Hartington to Millers Dale | 12.6 miles |

Out from Hartington we walked uphill through hilltop fields with good views over the Dove Valley. Once at the top we headed downhill for a while, over pastureland and river meadows to the ruins of Pilsbury Castle.

After the castle we were on an old packhorse road to Crowdecote: possibly this track was the original pathway to the Castle when it was in use.

There were fantastic views towards Dove Head and Chrome Hill as we'd approached Pilsbury Castle mound, and also as we came out of the village of Crowdecote towards Earl Sterndale.

Andy and Bob were amused by the name of the local public house – 'The Quiet Woman':

and the pub sign; which showed a lady with no head!!!

From Earl Sterndale the path went steeply up through a very pretty and well kept garden, before coming out on to the hillside.

Still heading uphill, and with views opening up, we climbed steeply for a while to Hindlow Quarry.

From the top it was a case of opposing views, as on the one hand we had spectacular scenery towards Chrome Hill, and on the other a gaping hole in the ground that was the Quarry.

From here we were now on a wide track, heavily rutted by quarry vehicles in the previous wet weather. Eventually the track levelled out and there were many butterflies and wild flowers here. On to the B5053, passing another quarry, and to the junction with the A515, where we found a bookshop in a building that we imagined had once been a garage. The bookshop was large and also had the benefit of refreshment, and so we spent a little while there before crossing the A515 and heading into Brierlow Dale: a little muddy where the cows had been, and then better walking again in Back Dale. Steep sided dry dales linking into Horseshoe Dale and then into the Nature Reserve of Deep Dale (SSSI). Here the path was narrow, rocky and slippery, sometimes shale rock, and overgrown, the woodland sections giving little sunlight. This was very hard-going for about a mile and a half which slowed our walking speed considerably. It was good to come out of this section, as we'd had to pass quarry workings and disused land containing quicksand and slurry at the far end of Deep Dale. In complete contrast, the track along Wye Dale and, briefly, on the Monsal trail, was easy walking and very pretty.

Walking uphill from the Monsal Trail, through a mass of wild flowers as we climbed, we headed up and over the hills to reach site.

A bite to eat, and retrieve Bob's car, and then from site we walked over the hills – beautiful views – down to Chee Dale and Chee Tor Tunnel on the Monsal Trail again now, which we followed to Miller's Dale old station: so that we can start walking tomorrow from Miller's Dale.

| Day 40 | Friday 27th July 2012 | Millers Dale to Upper Booth | 14.1 miles |

The stream through Millers Dale

From Millers Dale we entered into Monks Dale across a wooden bridge, then it was quite difficult going as the limestone rocky path was muddy and slippery: we had to pick our way for about two miles. It was pretty by the stream, but we had to walk at a reasonable and safe speed here.

Leaving Hay Dale

Then we came out into Peter Dale, which was more open, with cows, or evidence of cows, and some muddy sections at times, but it was easier going now in the main. We met up with the cows at the end of Peter Dale. After crossing the lane, we were on a grassy path into a wider grassy sloped valley. We stopped at 'Pat's Seat' (thank you to Pat!) for a drink, before going into Hay Dale which was lovely – easy walking and blue skies above us as the valley opened out. Gradually heading uphill we reached a wide track (Limestone Way), then carried on uphill for about half a mile to cross the A123.

Then still on the Limestone Way: through Brecktor, and uphill between dry stone walls on a good wide grassy track, we continued uphill to views of Mam Tor in the distance. From here we crossed high pasture land, with cattle and sheep, across to the top of Cave Dale. We had our lunch part way down Cave Dale and continued down this pretty valley, with its craggy limestone outcrops and Peveril Castle above, and into Castleton: slippery and wet rocks underfoot for part of the way here, as I found to my cost – the dry weather helped to dry out my shorts later as we walked!

The start of Cavedale, leading to Castleton

Refreshed by a cup of tea at a cafe in the town we headed towards the 'slipped road' below Mam Tor.

From here a track diagonally up the far side of the Hope Valley took us to Hollins Cross, where there were grand views: down into the Edale Valley, and across to Kinder Plateau and Kinder Scout ahead of us.

We followed the path down to Edale, all very beautiful in every direction: fantastic scenery!

Once down into the Edale Valley we were on a good path to the village, going under the Trans-Pennine Railway on the way.

In the village we had a photo taken of all four of us at the start of the Pennine Way (we're approximately 560 miles from Land's End now).

A good walk up a pack-horse road took us to a 'paved path' across open fields and out on to the hillside – what a stunning view.

Staying on the Pennine Way across the lower slopes to Upper Booth, we then had a little lane walking back to the car. Excellent walk in good weather. 14.1 good miles.

Day 41   Saturday 28th July 2012   Upper Booth to Torside   15.6 miles

From Upper Booth there was a little bit of lane walking before we reached our path. After crossing the stream on a grey stone bridge we started up 'Jacob's Ladder'. As expected, the path went steeply up – with steps up the first section.

Up from there to Kinder Low and Kinder Plateau to the trig point: very bare here, almost like a 'moon-scape', we then headed west along to Kinder Downfall. Fantastic views from here as far as the outer suburbs of Manchester. Almost a 360 degree panorama.

From Kinder Downfall we descended, eventually coming to a tough stony downhill path, and then on up to Mill Hill where we turned northwards across peat bog which had been paved; so a much easier way of crossing this moorland section than previously; and better for the preservation of the peat! About 2.5 miles of this terrain to cross the Snake Pass from Glossop to Sheffield. We were mainly on flagstones for a while, but then rocky, sandy and uneven terrain uphill onto Bleaklow, which was quite bleak moorland for the next three miles or so, broken by the stream of Hern Clough. Out then onto greener, heathery moorland going gradually down and then contouring above Teeside Clough down to the old railway alongside the Torside Reservoir and back to the car. The last hour or so we had some heavy, and cold, showers, but the day was mainly dry, with a fresh breeze up on the tops.

The next day, 29th July, we moved site to Mytholmroyd. Andy and I walked into Mytholmroyd, which was twice badly damaged by the June flooding, and many shops were under repair and renovation, so not much was open in this devastated town. My sister, Mary, arrived on site this evening and will join us in our walk tomorrow.

Day 42   Monday 30th July 2012   Torside Reservoir to near Redbrook Reservoir   14.2 miles

Bob's car to Redbrook and Mary's to Torside to start the walk. From Torside we re-joined the Pennine Way, in the rain at first, to cross the reservoir at the dam then walk uphill to cross a road and head up to Oaken Clough, the path running along the top of the crags and the Oakenclough Brook below us. Good views behind as we climbed.

We followed this path to the head of the valley and up to the moorland, which would have been really hard-going if it hadn't been for the flagstone path over the vast expanses of bog. The weather stayed fine, mostly, although in the morning the showers were never far away. By late afternoon the skies were clearing. We reached the summit and once over the crest we stopped to admire the panoramic view which stretched for miles: and decided that this was a great place to stop for lunch. Then down to cross the A62 and up again on a lane leading to a good track past another reservoir. To our right, we saw a deer enclosure along here, with some very young deer. To our left, a deep and green valley, with a fantastic waterfall at this point. A while further on we went down this valley to cross the stream and then continue steeply up the other side.

We had crossed many streams, which were quite high and tricky to cross without a drenching, and there were more to come.

Up on to moorland on mainly a flagstone path for a long while until we reached two reservoirs. We crossed between the two and made our way on a good track over the hill to the car park.

We decided to have a meal out after retrieving Mary's car from Torside, and after one disappointment of a closed pub, we eventually found a restaurant near the M1, which was excellent. Mary then left to drive home, and we went back to site. The 'satnav' in Bob's car indicated that we take the motorways back, and it was a very long drive – further than it needed to be we were sure (map-reading here would have been more successful than simply relying on the 'satnav').

| Day 43 | Tuesday 31st July 2012 | Near Redbrook Reservoir to Blackstone Edge Reservoir | 7.72 miles |

From Redbrook Reservoir Car Park we crossed the road and headed on a good stony path up to Standedge, from where there was a good view, with Manchester in the far distance.

Some large weathered rocks along Standedge were quite dramatic against the scenery beyond. From Standedge we headed across moorland and down to the Huddersfield Road, A640, then up across moorland onto White Hill.

From White Hill we went down again to cross the A672 at the Lancashire / West Yorkshire Border before heading down to a footbridge over the M62.

It seemed strange to be emerging from the wild moorland and being suddenly confronted with the hustle and bustle of commuting traffic and the busyness of people's lives. However we

were soon away from here onto Black Moor, over a small crest of a hill and down to a quieter spot for a lunch stop. Misty now, but still some visibility across the moorland, and up to Robin Hood's Bed, (rocky outcrop), then up still further in the low cloud

to Blackstone Edge, aptly named because of the line of black rocks along the edge of the hill at the top. Views obscured by cloud today, but they emerged faintly occasionally and as we came down out of the low cloud visibility improved.

Downhill to the Aiggin Stone (a medieval marker stone) on the moor and then diagonally down to a water leat. Crossing the leat by a bridge we then made our way down to the A58 (Roman Road) alongside Blackstone Edge Reservoir.

Day 44　　Wednesday 1st August 2012　　Blackstone Edge Reservoir to　　14.0 miles
Clough Foot and Gorpal Reservoir

Starting walking by Blackstone Edge Reservoir we were on a good Water Board Track along the 'dam' side of the reservoir, and then, still on a good track, to Light Hazzles Edge – a group of rocks: one with a beautifully lettered poem in gold on the rockface.

From there we were alongside Light Hazzles Reservoir, White Holme Reservoir and then Warland Reservoir.

Open moorland, and with views down to Littleborough on the west side. We made good time along here, reaching Warland Reservoir in 50 minutes (3.4 mph walking average).

We turned east briefly alongside Warland's Drain and then north over moorland, with grass and some rocky outcrops, to reach a view ahead to Studely Pike Monument: standing high above Todmorden and Hebden Bridge in the Calder Valley.

We had excellent views and it was good walking on firm moorland tracks up to Higher Moor and the Monument. From here we turned east, downhill on a grassy track, before heading north again alongside newly cultivated fields. A little stickier here in the cow field, but soon we were out on Edge End Moor and down a farm track (tarmac later) to the Rochdale Canal, west of Hebden Bridge, and also the River Calder (which flooded the valley twice in June this year).

After this, a very steep uphill on a stony, narrow path between gardens, fields and cottages, with superb views back to Studely Pike Monument beyond the wild flowers along our path. A narrow, muddy track with brambles, nettles and bracken followed before emerging out on moorland fields to a lane, which we crossed and headed toward Badger Fields Farm. We stopped for lunch at Pry Hill: with great views back to Studely Pike Monument, before heading up over the hill and then down between stone walls on a narrow, slippery, stony, overgrown path to reach Golden Clough.

View back to Studely Pike Monument as we climbed out of Hebden Bridge

This was a very pretty valley with the path taking us down to the stone bridge over Golden Clough. A steep path up and over from there gave us good views back, and when we reached a lane there was a welcome sign mentioning Hot Drinks, 200 yards left, so we deviated briefly to take advantage of a cup of tea and cake at 'May's Aladdin's Cave': the best stocked village shop we'd ever seen. Then back on route still heading up to Clough Head Hill. The scenery here was reminiscent of the Exmoor hills and valleys, and we enjoyed a mostly good path, some flagstones across boggy sections, and great views all the way across the moor and down to Clough Foot, passing Gorple Lower Reservoir, before reaching Graining Water, where there were two bridges across the streams. A very pretty spot with rowan trees. Then a short climb up and across some sheep fields to the road and a short walk to the car.

We started walking today at 9.15 am and finished walking at 3.15 pm, having had two stops, lunch and a cup of tea in that time. A really lovely day's walking altogether, setting a lively pace. We even had curlews to see and hear today, and a red deer back at site later.

Day 45 Thursday 2nd August 2012 Clough Foot to Ponden Reservoir 6 miles

After moving site to Gargrave, near Skipton, we set off to walk again. From Clough Foot we progressed uphill on a track and then on a tarmac driveway to Walshaw Dean Lower Reservoir. We crossed at the dam and then walked along the side of the reservoir on a bracken and rhododendron lined track next to a water leat on our right, continuing up to, and halfway along, Middle Reservoir before heading up onto the moors.

A steep climb then up to Dean Stones Edge on the moorland path: heather in abundance here but not yet in flower. We crossed the moor – Withins Height End – on a flagstone path in much of this section, the track taking us down to Top Withens Farmhouse: rumoured to be Emily Bronte's 'Wuthering Heights', where we stopped to admire the views and to have a drink.

Miles of moorland in each direction and a view to Haworth.

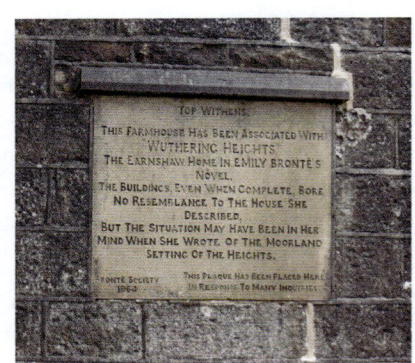

Coming down from there on a good wide track we were in 'Bronte' Country, the signposts were also in Japanese and Arabic in this tourist area.

We turned off the Haworth path, heading downhill at first and then across the lower slopes of Stanbury Moor to reach Ponden Reservoir. A section of lane walking here and then up and over a hill and down to a muddy section to get to the bridge, which we crossed. A path from here took us across fields and then steeply up to Dean Clough and to Crag Bottom.

Through fields, with woodland on our left, before reaching the lane where we'd parked the car. Good weather for all of today's walk, although rain had been forecast.

Day 46   Friday 3rd August 2012   Ponden to East Marton   13.7 miles

From Crag Bottom, via Crag Top, along the lane and then up on reedy marshy ground alongside a wall up Thornton Hill. Then out on to more open hillside, with some boggy, peaty sections amongst the heather, grasses and bilberries, still heading uphill until we reached the top of Bare Hill: and what a view was to be had, across to the Yorkshire Dales – absolutely stunning scenery and well worth the climb.

Down across Icknorshaw Moor for a couple of miles with good views all the way and on a better, sandier track. Once down we turned alongside a wall and on more marshy ground, with marsh grasses abundant here, we were passing little huts placed here and there. A young lad was on the wooden roof of one of these huts, painting, and Lynne and I asked what the huts were for: they were the accommodation for shooting parties to stay in overnight before rising at dawn for the grouse shooting – Glorious 12th and all that (but not so glorious for the grouse).

We then took a track across lovely sheep-grazed hillside, with beautiful views at Eller Hill. Then passing the top of a small waterfall, on a good wide track, to Icknorshaw where we crossed the A6068, pausing here for a drink stop at a shelter, with a good view down to the village.

Down through this village and up the other side of the valley and generally uphill from there across fields to Lothersdale, some on a green lane.

Pretty wild flowers here. Stopped for coffee at the 'Hare and Hounds'.

After this we headed uphill to heathery moorland and Pinhaw Beacon trig point, where there were amazing 360 degree panoramic views: all stunning scenery. Down from here, still on heather clad moorland, with more bilberries, we stopped to have lunch alongside the track. A beautiful view from here to Earby across the valley to our next village on the Pennine Way, Thornton-in-Craven. Across pasture land and then some more gentle hill walking past farms (and one very handsome cockerel) to the Leeds and Liverpool Canal to walk along the towpath to East Marton.

From Bridge 162 our route took us past a cafe where we stopped for ice cream before making our way to the car.

Weather today was again dry, although there were dark clouds and showers around, but we were fortunate to miss these in this very warm day, hot at times, with only a heavy shower back at site this evening.

Day 47   Saturday 4th August 2012   East Marton to Malham Tarn   14.8 miles

From East Marton we headed across sheep pasture land, several fields, going up gently at first, then steeper up Scaleber Hill, before heading down to the pretty village of Gargrave: we had a good view of the village church for a while before reaching the village.

There was an old-fashioned sweet shop in Gargrave so we *had* to go in and *re-live our youth* by indulging in buying sweets from large jars: the sweets being measured out in ounces!! We settled on fudge, sherbet lemons, liquorice and chocolate raisins. (We needed the energy, didn't we, for this last day of walking?)

Several fields of cows now in the hilly countryside as we headed uphill for quite a while before reaching the village of Airton. Walking then downhill to the River Aire, which we followed to the village, we stopped briefly, during a heavy shower, at the tea-room to indulge in cream scones and a cup of hot chocolate or coffee, thinking that we would surely walk all these calories off today!

Andy and Meg, Bob and Lynne on hill before Airton

On leaving it was still raining so the waterproofs had to go on, albeit not for long. Then the sun came out and it stayed dry and very warm as we headed to Malham, and Malham Cove, on gradually rising ground after we'd followed the river for quite a while. The view of Malham Cove was impressive as we approached Malham Village and here we were 'forced' to slow our pace as we met the gamut of tourists here as we approached the Cove.

There was great excitement as we arrived at the Cove as there were sightings of peregrine falcons nesting here, with three chicks, so several bird-spotters there with their cameras and binoculars. As we climbed the limestone steps to the limestone pavement above the cove, Bob and Lynne were fortunate to get a glimpse of one of the adult peregrine falcons in flight.

We had our picnic lunch with a grand view of the limestone pavement and the countryside below and beyond.

Sitting in the very hot sunshine it was a lovely spot, but we had to keep going before the forecast heavy rain got to us. Heading to Malham Tarn via Ing Scar: a beautiful steep sided limestone valley, we were then on grassy paths across the limestone moorland.

On reaching Malham Tarn, there was an ice-cream van, so we stopped for a while with our ice creams, but not for long, as there was thunder rolling around and dark clouds approaching, so we headed round to the far side of the Tarn: walking at a good pace.

We managed to get a photo of the four of us at Malham Tarn: courtesy of a passing walker, and so finished this year's three weeks of walking for LeJog. Happy to have reached our destination and happy also to reach the car just before the rains came down. 243.4 miles since Chipping Campden, 660.4 miles since Land's End.

Day 48   Monday 23rd October 2012   Malham Tarn to Horton in Ribblesdale   11.2 miles

Travelling north yesterday morning, encountering mist and fog on the way, we emerged into sunshine just before Scotch Corner on the A1. Turning left off the A1 onto the A66 toward Brough and Penrith we travelled as far as Bowes, where we turned off the main road and through the village to the Certified Site we'd booked at Ivy House Farm.

Lovely views from the site, and once we'd both set up we took a walk down the valley to the River Greta and then back through the village past Bowes Castle. Before reaching there we walked up the 'Wynd' where we saw an interesting stone gateway with carved figures and a lion. While we were wondering about it a gentleman came out of his cottage through the said gateway, and explained that in 1842 a circus had come to Bowes: a lion had escaped from its cage and gone through the village, terrifying the inhabitants. A group of farmers had got together with any weapons they could find and cornered the lion in the 'Wynd', where we were stood, and managed to get it back into its cage, without it having harmed anyone. Hence the carved lion in the gateway!

Back at site we had our evening meal and then a brief meeting at Bob and Lynne's to finalise the first day of walking. We were to drive to Horton in Ribblesdale: about 1 hour 15 mins away, and then take a taxi at 8.50 am to Malham Tarn, where we'd finished walking in the summer.

Day 48 of the walk

This meant rising at 6.30 am: which we did, leaving the site at 7.30 am. All went to plan apart from the weather, which was foggy at first with low cloud over the fells. Undaunted we set off, after taking the 'obligatory', and, by now, 'legendary' photos of the four of us at the start of this next section of the walk (LeJog).

The beginning of the walk was in a dry valley, with the grassy path running alongside a stone wall. Visibility wasn't great, so there were no views to speak of. Further on the grassy slopes changed to moorland paths and an uphill path, steadily taking us up to Fountains Fell: several 'false' summits before reaching the top. We took a photo of us in the mist by the trig point

and then took the path down to the road by Dale Head Farm (stopping for a 'flapjack' courtesy of Lynne this time). We followed the road for about a mile: we were now beneath the cloud so there were some views of the very pretty valleys and hills in their autumn colours.

However, the cloud was still shrouding Pen-y-Ghent: our next destination, and once we'd walked uphill for a while along the ridge we were once again in misty low cloud and there was a strong easterly wind making progress slower than otherwise. Quite an arduous climb, with two sections of 'rock scrambling' before reaching the summit where, once again, 'trig point in the mist' photos were taken. We found shelter out of the wind and rain and had our lunch – much appreciated and earned by now we felt.

The way off Pen-y-Ghent was more gentle than the ascent and, once we were out of the cloud, views emerged, and it was a pleasant walk down to a green lane (Horton Scar Lane) and into Horton in Ribblesdale. The cameras came out for the autumn colours: and views at last.

Once in the village we had a welcome stop for a cup of tea at the Pen-y-Ghent Cafe on the Pennine Way, where we signed the Pennine Way Log Book. When we ordered the tea it was sold in *pint* mugs. Lynne was convinced that she'd not manage a *pint* of tea, but a short while later she was surprised to find she'd finished it after all!! (as we had too!)

A short distance to walk to Bob's car and a drive to Hawes to get provisions before heading back to site, The weather conditions worsened as we drove back, with mist and rain preventing any views.

But we were happy that we'd achieved today's section of the walk, 11.2 miles walked – a pity about the lack of views from Pen-y-Ghent: we consoled ourselves with the thought that the weather hadn't been all bad, and we had, in the main, kept dry and warm.

Day 49   Tuesday 24th October 2012   Horton in Ribblesdale to Hawes   14.9 miles

We left the site at 8.00 am to drive to Hawes, to leave our car there, and then travelled in Bob and Lynne's car to Horton in Ribblesdale. There was low cloud again today but not so low as yesterday, and as we approached Horton in Ribblesdale there was an emerging view of Pen-y-Ghent. We stopped the car and took some photos before reaching our destination for the start of today's section from Horton to Hawes.

Leaving Horton on a walled green lane we headed uphill for quite some time, getting better views of Pen-y-Ghent as we ascended. It was pleasant walking, not too cold, and dry, although rather grey. The tops were still, in the main, covered in thin cloud. On looking across to Pen-y-Ghent, at one point, it appeared as if the thin cloud was cascading down it: almost like a waterfall.

We passed some impressive 'sink holes' on our way as we walked along a wide track to Ling Nature Reserve. Passing the impressive steep sided rocky gorge: the stream cascading down as a waterfall here, we then headed on down to join the stream (Ling Gill Beck) at a bridge beyond the end of the gorge.

From here there was a steady ascent on a good wide track for several miles up to Cam End and Cam High Road where the Pennine Way joins the Dales Way for a mile or so.

Good view of the Ribblehead Viaduct, although it was still quite dull.

However, not as dull as it was to be as we ascended up to Cam Fell: the mist came down and we walked for several miles in heavy mist with no views for about six miles. We had our heads, and the rest of us, in the clouds for quite a while, and it was just a question of keeping going, still heading uphill for several miles.

We eventually reached a stone wall, at Kidhow Gate, where we could shelter from the wind and have our lunch. We were very hungry by then and enjoyed our lunch stop.

We took a group photo of us enjoying life, and then headed off, still on the Pennine Way, across to Rottenstone Hill, all the while feeling quite isolated from the reality of the outside world in the continuing mist down to Hawes.

It was a quite some distance before we came out of the mist – in fact we were only about a mile from Hawes, on the approach to Gaudy Lane, when the surrounding countryside could be seen. We made the most of it and appreciated the views around us as we descended to Hawes.

By the time we reached the car we had walked 14.9 miles, so we could be forgiven for driving to the Creamery to purchase cheeses: a Wensleydale speciality, although there was no cup of tea to be had as it was approaching closing time and the café was not open.

However, we purchased cheese and fruit cake before Andy and Bob drove back to Horton to collect Bob's car. In the meantime, Lynne and I went into the town to get food etc. When Andy and Bob returned we had fish and chips for our supper before heading back to Bowes and our caravans.

A hot shower: and more food, and we felt 'human' again, and, hopefully, ready for tomorrow's section from Hawes to Keld.

Day 50 **Friday 27th October 2012** **Hawes to Keld** **13 miles**

What yesterday lacked, we had today in abundance: spectacular views, good paths generally, and dry feet. We also had some sunshine at times today.

However, there was a distinct temperature change today: as we drove to Hawes the temperature fluctuated between 1 and 0 degrees and there was a cold wind. So a bright autumn day to start the walk – well, wintry really – as there were sleety showers around.

From Hawes we took the path to Great Shunner Fell: a long ascent on good paths all the way, with views back to Wensleydale and beyond to the impressive Ingleborough, now out of the cloud. As we went higher there was a dusting of snow on the ground in places and there was ice on the wet ground. After two and a half hours walking uphill we arrived at the summit of Great Shunner Fell just as the sleet came down and we made use of the stone cross-shaped shelter there to have our hot drinks and a flapjack. While there a young lad came from the opposite direction and he stopped to talk to us: he was walking John O' Groats to Land's End. He was fresh out of university and hadn't much walking experience and he told us how he'd started out without proper walking boots and had to order some – and had walked part of the way in flip flops! He'd also gone up to his armpits in a bog a few days back. He was full of confidence and determination, despite no maps – relying on GPS – and in the temperatures we had today he was realising gloves might be a good idea! The temperature at the top was -2 or -3 degrees.

As we went our separate ways, we descended Great Shunner Fell toward Thwaite. There was a bitingly cold wind and we kept moving until we were out of the wind before stopping for lunch. The moorland on the way down was full of gold and orange and pink colours – the grasses and reeds were very pretty, and a contrast against the dark peat.

Part of the way was flag-stone path, although there were sections where we had to detour because of the boggy conditions. We had views opening out down to the valley where Thwaite Beck led to the village of Thwaite, and beyond that the village of Muker: Straw Beck joining the Swale at the village of Muker. As we descended further the sun came out on the valley below and it was really pretty.

We had lunch sat on a bank next to the stony track and at first it was sunny. When the sun went in there was a distinct change of temperature and we quickly got ready to walk the short distance to Thwaite. From Thwaite we took the path uphill past many field barns and out on to the open fells: a more gentle landscape now compared to the morning's high moorland fells, with superb views down Swaledale in both directions, with beautiful autumn colours enhancing the scene. As we walked toward Keld we were on the opposite side of the valley to the Coast to Coast Path and, having done this walk previously, we were spotting the landmarks: Swinner Gill Lead Mines, Crackpot Hall and Gunnerside, as we walked.

The path was quite challenging in places, rocks and scree obstructing the path, and we had to pick our way a bit. The views made up for these difficulties and, even though there was a cold wind to begin with, as we descended the wind lessened and we found ourselves in sight of Keld. A short walk on a better path now past the waterfall at Keld and back to our waiting car.

Day 51 **Wednesday October 24ᵗʰ 2012** **Keld to Bowes** **13.1 miles**

We started the day by leaving our car at Keld to walk to site at Bowes. Arriving at Keld we re-lived the time when we'd walked through and camped there on Wainwright's Coast to Coast Walk.

The autumn colours were magnificent and the waterfall at Keld worth many photos: which of course we took. With great reluctance, and regret, we left Keld with its memories of the great Coast to Coast route, which was tempting us greatly: *Change course and carry on to Richmond?*, particularly as the route up on the Pennine Way seemed to be heading for the

low clouds; and the Coast to Coast path was still in sunshine, but carry on we must, to follow Andy and Bob who were waiting for Lynne and me to finish our 'love affair' with Keld and to join them along the Pennine Way up along the fell side along Stonesdale Beck.

At first we had views along the valley but as we rose higher we were once again in the mist, and increasing wetness of the inclement weather, on a good track up to the moorland over to Tan Hill Inn – the highest in Britain.

We were within a few hundred yards of the Inn but couldn't see it until, suddenly, out of the mist, there it was before us – a very welcome sight, especially as it was open. On leaving there a little while later we were surprisingly content with our lot, despite the low cloud and overall wetness: no doubt attributable to the excellent warm Inn, hot chocolate (with cream and syrup) or coffee, a lovely coal fire burning in the grate where we sat around, and the added indulgence of a Snickers bar each. We are so easily pleased!!

The Tan Hill Inn emerging from the mist

Walking the alternative route over the moorland on a lane, rather than the 'dangerous (according to the guide book on the Pennine Way) path over the bogs', we made our way downhill, the silence only being interrupted by the cackling laughter of grouse as they took off occasionally before winging their way across the moorland, looking every bit like tiny Hercules aircraft, with their large bodies under a slim looking wingspan.

Eventually we turned off the road, after passing a bridge at Mirk Fell Gill: aptly named in today's weather conditions, and were on a track which led after a while down to the river.

We passed a farm, the first building since the Inn at Tan Hill, and then crossed to the river bridge, with difficulty at one flooded gateway, to reach a picnic spot at Sleightholme Beck for lunch (only Andy and I had forgotten to put our sandwich box in the rucksack – thank goodness for the previous snack at the Inn, and an unexpected extra Snickers bar that Bob had 'won' at the Inn).

We were sat on a rock next to the bridge, which after a while began to feel cold, so we headed on our way alongside the river: losing the path briefly, but quickly correcting ourselves by climbing up a steep bank to where we should have been.

We soon started to hear the sound of traffic on the A66, which meant we were nearing the 'Bowes Loop' of the Pennine way, which we took, going parallel to the A66, though at a reasonable distance away, and later alongside the River Greta, to reach our site back at Bowes.

Still wet and rather soggy, we were pleased to be back at our dry and warm caravans.

After a welcome cup of tea, Bob drove Andy back to Keld to retrieve our car.

Day 52   **Thursday 26th October 2012**   **Bowes to Middleton in Teesdale**   **12.6 miles**

When we awoke this morning the weather looked more promising with higher cloud level and some breaks in the cloud. We set off from site uphill on a lane passing disused Ministry of Defence sites, and our walking was accompanied by the sound of gunfire from the nearby army firing range. This was after two miles of walking today which meant that we had now walked 700 miles since Land's End: perhaps the gunfire was in salute to that?

After a while we turned on to a track over moorland and then down to Deepdale Beck in the valley of Deep Dale. The thatched farmhouse by the bridge crossing looked as though it was right out of 'Lark Rise to Candleford', apart from its setting in the moorland. We carried on up the other side of Deep Dale, on boggy paths, picking our way.

The path rose and fell as we went up over marshy moor and down boggy dale for several miles, until over the rise we saw the landmark of Goldsborough: standing proud at the top of the next hill.

We walked below this rocky crag and then uphill again. Over the crest of the hill there was a good panoramic view of Balderdale and the three reservoirs: Balderhead Reservoir, Blackston and Hury reservoirs. We reached the road in the valley bottom and took the path down to East Friar House, where there were good views along the valley.

We crossed between Balderhead and Blackston Reservoirs to a Nature Reserve: many sheep down by the water's edge, and then uphill to Hannah's Meadow – a most impressive curly horned ram there with two lady friends. Uphill on a road to begin with and then off on the moor – very wet and boggy conditions for a while over and down to Kelton Bottom – extremely wet, muddy and many springs making the going challenging. It seemed as though the muddy fields in Warwickshire this summer were a mere preliminary training for the mud we encountered today - I think we all got wet feet by the end of the walk. After the dubious delights of Kelton Bottom we crossed a very awkward field to a stone stile: on a slope and very muddy. Encounters with previous muddy fields came to our minds here, and it took quite a bit of negotiating a way through and over to the road. On tarmac now down to the Grassholme Reservoir, where once across the causeway we reached a picnic site next to the water.

We were very pleased to stop for a while and enjoy lunch before heading uphill once more to Crossthwaite Common. We were now into the lower fells and green pasture and although still muddy at times, it was nothing like the boggy wetness of the morning's walking. The views opened out more as we reached the top and although it was not a bright day we could see quite a distance.

On reaching the top of the Common we had a magnificent view of Middleton in Teesdale: grey stone houses nestling among the autumn trees, the fells surrounding the town. Dotted around the surrounding hillsides were white cottages, so a very picturesque end to our day and a welcome contrast to the bleak and barren moorland we had walked over today. The walk down to Middleton in Teesdale was very pretty, the route crossing the river just before the main part of the town. By this time we all felt we

deserved tea and cakes, so after taking off disgustingly mucky waterproof trousers and wet boots, and having a welcome change of dry footwear, we took ourselves off to the nearest tea room!!!

| Day 53 | Saturday 28th October 2012 | Middleton in Teesdale to Cow Green Reservoir | 14.4 miles |

When Andy said – 'There's snow outside' – I thought he was joking but, sure enough, an inch of snow had fallen overnight, and there was also a cold wind. In the clear skies yesterday evening we had expected a good frost, but had never thought that it would snow.

Driving to Cow Green to leave our car there was therefore a slower journey in the wintry conditions, but, interestingly, there was less snow after we'd gone through Middleton in Teesdale, but ice on the roads meant even more cautious driving. Leaving our car by the reservoir we then travelled with Bob and Lynne to Middleton to start our walk. There was a very raw feel to the day as we started walking: a bitter cold wind, but also a very clear sky and sunshine.

The walk started along the River Tees going northwards, and the autumn colours against the snow made for a very pretty scene – Lynne and I soon got our cameras out. The Pennine Way took us up to Low Force Waterfalls, which were very dramatic: we sat and admired the scene when we had a break mid-morning. The colours reflected in the water from the autumn trees were fantastic.

Going on along the riverside we came across two life-sized sheep sculptures, which Andy and Bob sat astride for a photo shoot – as though they were 'sheep' racing!!!

On once more, and we soon arrived at the next waterfall: High Force. Dramatic in a different way to Low Force with its series of falls, the river at High Force came down a huge drop to the river below it, the dark rocks making it quite spectacular. From High Force the scenery changed to low moorland with juniper trees on the lower slopes. We crossed over this juniper covered moorland and back down to the riverside where we stopped to have our picnic lunch.

As the river course went round a large bend, the Pennine Way left the riverside to go over the hillside to join the river further along, and

we found the scenery quite different as we approached down hill: grassy moorland, with white farm cottages dotted on the hillsides, the Tees flowing through a wide valley here. Crossing vast expanses of pasture land, with herds of cattle across this wide valley, we followed the river upstream, and as we went further upstream the valley gradually narrowed and the path became more difficult with rocks and boulders to negotiate at the lower edges of scree.

A bit of scrambling was needed here. As we approached Cauldron Snout we could hear the water crashing down well before we saw it. And when we did see it, it quite outshone the other waterfalls of the day. A dramatic end to the day, especially so, as we then had to climb up rocks alongside this waterfall right to the top to reach our destination for this section: the dam at the end of Cow Green Reservoir, from which the Tees flows.

A spectacular end to this year's walking LeJog and the Pennine Way. The weather today bright and clear, although 'bracing'! A great sense of achievement: 737 miles walked since Land's End. We celebrated this evening by having a meal at The Fox and Hounds at the village of Cotherstone before finishing the day at Bob and Lynne's to talk about the next section next year!!

BOOTS OFF!!

| Day 54 | Sunday 14th July 2013 | Cow Green Reservoir to Knock | 14.0 miles |

When we left the site at 8.10 am it was so misty you wouldn't have known that there were any fells to climb. Leaving our car at Knock, we then drove to Cow Green Reservoir in Bob's car, going via Brough and then turning to go to Middleton in Teesdale, up the Teesdale Valley where we'd walked last year, and then up to Cow Green Reservoir. As we approached, the sun came through the mist and by the time we'd parked up and got ready to walk the sun had come through and there was blue sky. With the promise of a hot and sunny day there was a very different view to be had than when we were here in the snow and ice back in late October of 2012.

We made good time down the lane to the bridge above Cauldron Snout, where a group photo was taken *(more about that later)*. Pleasant walking, uphill, but not overly steep, with Maize Beck on our left – not much water running into the Tees from here today – and, across the valley, the hills of the firing range. We crossed the Beck on a high footbridge after about four miles: interesting bedrock in the Beck which looked as though it had been cut into squares. We then had the Beck on our right as we approached High Cup Plain and High Cupgill Head. It was a gorgeous sunny day, with a light breeze, very quiet apart from the various birdsong: skylarks, curlews, lapwings and grouse. The geological spectacular that is High Cup Nick was superb – with a fantastic view across towards the Lake District, Howgill Fells and the Yorkshire Dales. A vast panorama spread before us beyond the U-shaped valley of High Cup Nick, with its rocky outcrops of Whin Sill on the ridge.

We could easily have stayed here all day, just soaking up the views, but after lunch here we had to leave and make our way toward the village of Dufton.
Still with amazing views ahead, and much discussion as to 'Was that Whernside?' or 'Is that the Lake District over there, or Howgill Fells?', we made our way down to a gentler landscape and into Dufton.

We found refreshment at the pub, a good cup of tea was had in the beer garden, and more great views up toward what we've nicknamed 'the golfball' on top of the ridge where we shall be walking tomorrow. From Dufton an enclosed track took us generally uphill though the lower farmland fells, passing Dufton Pike on our right and then by Knock Pike. Along this path we saw cows paddling in a large pond – they must have been very hot today.

After crossing more farmland and then on a pretty walled path, with foxgloves, we arrived at the village of Knock and our car. Back to site for a cup of tea and cake before setting off in our car to Cow Green to retrieve Bob's car. *Here we took a second group photo as my earlier photo this morning had somehow been deleted off the camera.* From there we drove over the bleak moorland down to Garrigill, to leave Bob's car there overnight, and then drove back to site in ours, passing the most spectacular scenery: across to the Lake District mountains and even further to the Solway Firth and Dumfries and Galloway. The views really were breathtaking – a camera just can't do them justice – the distant mountains a pale grey or blue in the background, with the patchwork of fields and lower fells catching the evening sunlight making the most of the gentle greens and yellows in the vast landscape. Simply stunning!

Day 55   **Monday 15th July 2013**   **Knock to Garrigill**   **15.3 miles**

Today we awoke to blue sky and sunshine, so it promised to be another hot and sunny day. Setting off walking from Knock we started up along a really pretty path: with foxgloves on either side and with the high fells beyond. We set off uphill: the main feature of the first third of today's walking, initially up past Knock Pike and beyond, in very warm temperatures, until we finally reached Knock Fell, where there was a very welcome breeze. With good views behind us: over what was Westmorland in days gone by, and towards the Lake District, we had every reasonable excuse during our climb to stop every so often and admire the scenery. *Today the Lake District*

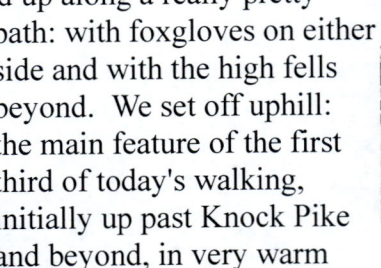

was cloudy, and misty, so not so clear as yesterday. Eventually we reached the top and headed across to Great Dun Fell, with its huge 'golf-ball' feature and masts. By now there was a very definite strong breeze and we needed to put extra layers of clothing on.

Down from Great Dun Fell and then *up again* to Little Dun Fell was a struggle in the breeze, and once on Little Dun Fell, after a 'necessary' *(to me)* flapjack stop, there was less steep walking over the top before heading down, yet again, to start the great ascent of Cross Fell. We were told that today would prove challenging, and it was!!

Andy and Lynne at the Cairn on Knock Fell

Bob and Andy heading for Great Dun Fell while Lynne takes a photo of the cotton grass flowering

A 'close up' of the top of Great Dun Fell taken as we were climbing up to Knock Fell

Great Dun Fell towards Cross Fell

Heading down to the Yad Stone

Up to Cross Fell, where we took a group photo before scurrying for shelter from the now very cool and stiff breeze, to have our lunch. We then started on the descent, some of which was on flagstone paths across the bogs with some lovely patches of white cotton grass brightening up the moorland scenery. Eventually, after quite a long descent, we reached a stony track going past Greg's hut, (bothy) after turning in an easterly direction at the Yad stone. From here we were contouring on the stony, gravelly track past old mine workings. Gradually heading in a more northerly direction we followed the path all the way down to Garrigill, some seven miles away. The moorland scenery around us was vast, with no trees, just high moorland.

Bob bringing ice cream from the village shop in Garrigill

We found the track walking quite relentless and we were all quite tired when we reached Garrigill (or even before that if we're honest!) However, the day was dry and sunny, although we had a little thin cloud on Cross Fell, and the ground conditions were dry so we were thankful not to have had to endure bad weather for this section of the walk, as that would have been a challenge too far!

Back at the car in Garrigill, Bob and Andy found the village shop and brought back ice creams which were very welcome, before we set off via Alston, for bread and fuel, back to the site.

We were again rewarded with stunning scenery and panoramic views of the Lake District and beyond as we travelled back to site. We walked 15.3 miles today.

Day 56   Tuesday 16th July 2013   Garrigill to Whitley Castle (Roman Fort)   7.3 miles

We had to move site today and were on the road before 9 am. The traffic was light on the M6 and we made good time to the Carlisle Junction, where we turned east on the A69 to Bampton and on to Gilsland, near Haltwhistle in Northumberland. Once we'd set up camp, we had coffee and then took our car to Whitley Castle and then Bob's car on to Garrigill to start walking toward Alston.

It was a completely different type of scenery today, with the first part being along the banks of the River South Tyne to Alston. There was a fine array of wild flowers, including orchids, along the bank. We saw a curlew in a field near the river and later on in the walk: just before Alston, a red squirrel.

A passing walker offered to take a photo of all four of us: seen here on a bridge as we crossed the River South Tyne between Garrigill and Alston.

We sat on the steps of the Alston War Memorial for our picnic lunch before carrying on through some beautiful pasture land, which with its many mature trees looked as though it was part of a large 'estate', towards the A689, which we crossed to go uphill to the higher Northumbrian fells where there were wonderful views across very green pasture, conifer plantations and the higher moorland. Stone walls and cottages on the various farm land.

We headed downhill to Gilderdale Burn, crossing it by a wooden bridge, then uphill on Isaac's Tea Trail: which joins the Pennine Way here, and over lush green fields to the Roman Fort of Whitley Castle. Down to a farm and then through some shady woodland back to the car.

It was very warm again today, but with some cloud and a little welcome breeze up on the higher fells. So, *another dry day* of walking and it looks like it will stay that way for a while at least.

We drove into Alston after the walk and while the men dealt with collecting Bob's car Lynne and I did a little food shopping. The men joined us and we had a cup of tea at the nearby tea room before heading back to site.

This evening we got together to play some music.

Red Squirrel seen just before we reached Alston

Day 57   Wednesday 17th July 2013   Whitley Castle (Roman Fort) to Gilsland   16 miles

We started today's walk heading toward the South Tyne Railway at Kirkhaugh.

We saw lapwings and curlews and, surprisingly, an oyster catcher as we walked, and also many wild flowers.

Along the river for some of the route we went through gentle, pretty countryside, leaving the river to go through the village of Slaggyford where we stopped to have a drink under the shelter of an oak tree on the village green. From here we headed uphill and away from the river, passing a very attractive chapel conversion with a lovely garden.

Down to Knar Burn and then up to Merry Knowe farm before going downhill to Burnstones, where we hoped to get a drink at the pub, but we were too early – it opened at 12 noon and we arrived just before 11 am. So we re-traced our steps and the route took us up to the moorland – along the edge of Glendue Fell,

Quite bleak up here, with mainly boggy grassland, but today at least it was dry in this hot weather.

We were heading down to the road to Glendue Burn and this was very pretty with a footbridge over. We were very tempted to paddle in the cool water, but decided against it as we had quite a trek ahead of us still.

Uphill again to the moorland, and then after a while another mile or so we were heading down hill with wonderful panoramic views across Northumberland and we could now see Hadrian's Wall in the far distance.

The land was quite different now as we reached the bottom of the hill, and we had a good two miles or more across flat land which was very dry and parched. Just before reaching Hartley Burn we came across a shady spot to have lunch under some trees.

Uphill again and on to the hillside passing a farm cottage where there were two pigs grazing. The owners of the cottage kindly asked if we had enough water in this hot weather: we had, but it was kind of them to offer; and we carried on uphill to Hartleyburn Common *(North Side)*: another stretch of bleak moorland, and we lost the views for a while. In wet weather this would have been a most unpleasant part of the walk, and it was clear from the now dried up moss that normally this would have been very boggy. As it was it was a little relentless, with only rough moorland grass around. We managed to lose our way a little towards the end of this section as the path on the ground was very unclear with so many clumps of boggy reed and grasses to negotiate. However we managed, by using GPS and map references, to find our way back on route and we were soon on a firm track towards the A69 which we had to cross on the level. Once across we headed up and over the hill to Greenhead and then along the lane to site.

Day 58   Thursday 18th July 2013   Thirlwall Castle to Housesteads   11.7 miles

We took one car to our starting point today near Thirlwall Castle, and took the path going past some miners' cottages to a bridge over a stream and across to Thirlwall Castle: built from the stone from Hadrian's Wall before the importance of the Wall was recognised! The castle is now a ruin and today was enjoyed by nesting swifts who flew above us and then dived into their nesting holes in the castle wall. I tried to photograph them but didn't succeed – they fly at such a speed.

A little further on, and to reach the Wall, we had to walk uphill through a field of cows with calves: and the bull was just by the gate into the field. It was quite a large field too. In the event the cows were fine and hardly moved. Once up this field we were at Hadrian's wall and the views from the top were panoramic.

The path followed the wall, passing mile castles and turrets along the way as we made our way to Walltown Crags, Aesica Roman Fort, Cawfield Crags and Caw Gap.

I never thought I'd write in this log that it was *too hot,* (too wet, too windy, too cold and too steep we've had on many occasions since Land's End but never too hot!) but today proved me wrong.

It was really *very warm* today right from the start and as the day progressed we welcomed any breeze or patch of shade. Shade was difficult to come by with the wall on our left hand side (north) and the sun beating down on us on the south side. By lunchtime we only managed to get a little shade by finding a gap in the wall and to sit on the north side.

Views from our lunch stop - looking north to Northumberland

The views along the way were spectacular, and we met several people today doing the Hadrian's Wall Long Distance walk as well as day trippers out to enjoy the sunshine. Temperatures today were edging towards 30 degrees and we were in full sun. Much sun cream needed and we made sure we carried plenty of drinks with us.

At Sycamore Gap: so named because this is the only tree for many miles along the Wall, we had our flapjacks and a drink– a good excuse to spend time in the shade – before carrying on the walk as far as Housesteads, where the Pennine Way leaves Hadrian's Wall to go north.

I was amused by some nearby sheep, looking down on us as we walked – they were in a single, and regular line on the hillside.

However, today we stopped at Housesteads Roman Fort and had ice creams and cold drinks before heading down to the Visitor Centre, where we had to catch the bus back to Walltown. We walked from Walltown the ¾ mile back to the car. As we've now done 800 miles since Land's End we decided to celebrate and have a meal out. We drove to the Bull's Head in Haltwhistle and had a very enjoyable meal. Back to site it was still warm and we sat outside with a cup of tea before writing our logs, saving photos and getting lunches ready for tomorrow.

Day 59   Friday 19th July 2013   Housesteads to Bellingham   13.7 miles

Took Bob's car to Bellingham and ours back to Housesteads to start the walk. We started uphill to Hadrians Wall to go though the gap between Hotbank Crags *(aptly named for the end of yesterday's walking!!)* and Cuddy's Crags, to follow the Pennine Way across Ridley Common moorland, grazed by cattle and sheep, heading towards Kielder Forest Park.

A look back at Hadrian's Wall

We left Hadrian's Wall here: through the gate and across into Kielder Forest

In this summer's hot spell this was good walking, generally, though I imagine it would be awful in wet weather as this was marshland with the potential for bogs. After a mile or so we reached the woodland and we were on forest tracks to start with, then off through the woodland on smaller paths where we were plagued for quite a while with flies, and horseflies.

Once we were out in the open again crossing Haughton Common we stopped for a drink, and the flies weren't so bad after a while. Bob tried out his mosquito net hat at this point!

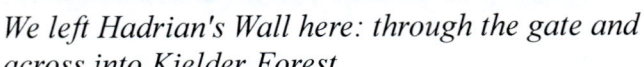

At the end of the common we were again in woodland, but this time without the flies, so more pleasant. There were plenty of wild flowers to look at on our way, and once out in the open again we were on moorland heading to a lane.

Along the lane were more wild flowers –

rosebay willowherb and meadowsweet together for several yards.

Crossing over farmland for a while on the lower moorland we came across a farm that provided 'serve yourself' refreshments: we had a cold drink and a cup of coffee before heading across more farmland. After passing a stone house in a beautiful setting and with lovely gardens we stopped on a grassy bank along the lane to have our lunch. Onwards on the lane and then a track across moorland and farms until we came to Shitlington Crags, at the end of an uphill climb across cowfields.

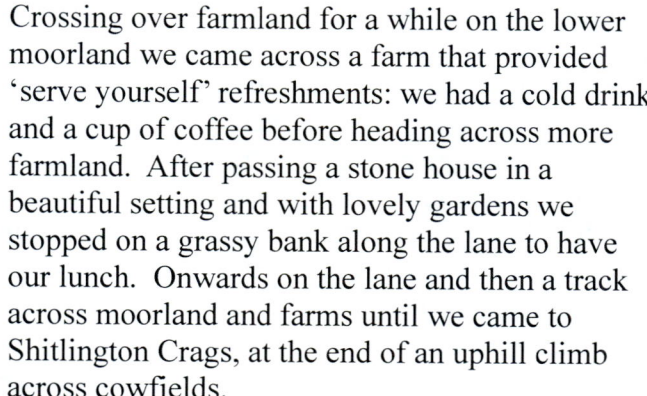

To our right in the next field were cows all facing us in a line at the top of the slope, as if they were wondering what on earth we were doing!

Up through the Crags on a rocky path and then a track uphill to a tall mast, then onward to a stile where we turned right on a track where there were lovely views to the south.

We turned north again on the track and headed across the lower moorland through meadows until we reached the road into Bellingham. We were on a footpath alongside the road for a while until we reached the 'Bellingham' sign.

From there the Pennine Way took us along the banks of the River North Tyne into the town centre, where we stopped for refreshment at the Rocky Road Cafe: for *yet another* very welcome pot of tea and then ice cream.

Back to Housesteads to get our car and travel back to site.
We move site tomorrow up to Town Yetholm at the end of the Pennine Way.
Lynne and I went to pay our site fees and to get our LeJog forms signed.

Day 60 **Sunday 21st July 2013** **Bellingham to Byrness** **15.6 miles**

We drove to Byrness and then had a taxi from there to Bellingham, to start the walk. It was a cooler morning with cloud as we set off, and so much more pleasant walking today. After a short while in the town we started uphill on a road towards Hareshaw Common and then over moorland past Callerhues Crag, down to Hareshaw House and on to the bridge over Brockley Burn before heading uphill to Deer Play and Whitley Pike.

Reading about this section of the Pennine Way last evening the author warned of '*vast expanses of boggy moorland in the first half of the walk where you would be fortunate indeed to escape going thigh deep into the bog, and a monotonous second section through endless forestry tracks with no views for miles*'. Thus inspired we set off well prepared for what was to follow.

In this dry weather the fears of boggy ground proved unfounded and we were fortunate to keep our feet dry throughout. The moorland was beautiful, with large patches of cotton grass standing out well against the darker heather (not yet in flower). The views across the moor were vast, and with dry feet and good weather we made excellent progress. We had a stop after 4 miles to have a drink and after Whitley Pike we crossed a minor road before going up Padon Hill. It was quite steep here, but still a good dry path – Exmoor ponies grazing on the hill on our right: a long way from home!

Over the top of Padon Hill we had sight of the Kielder Forest plantations: it was a glorious spot in the sunshine and Bob decided that this was the place for our lunch stop. With reluctance 20 minutes later: as we were quite happy admiring the views, we set off again downhill to the plantation, and it was a steep climb for a while up to Brownrigg Head on the edge of the forest. From Brownrigg Head the cotton grass again was all around on the moorland and we had the forest on our left as we made our way down.

Then we were on Forestry Commission Tracks but there were still views as the plantation in the main was only a few years old and we could see the wooded hillsides for some distance. We were really stepping it out along this section and soon came to Redesdale and a picnic site, where we had flapjacks to keep us going. By this time we'd forgotten we'd ever had lunch: we were quite hungry and the flapjacks were very welcome.

We made the decision to walk a mile further than the car was parked: Bob and Andy nobly offered to walk the extra mile to collect it, so that we could be one mile further along the Pennine Way when we walk again. 15.6 miles walked today, in really lovely weather: the sun came out late morning and there was cloud around in the afternoon making temperatures comfortable today. And so Lynne and I were quite happy to wait, near the church at Byrness, for the men to arrive.

Day 61   Tuesday 23rd July 2013   Byrness to Windy Gyle   17.5 miles

It was cloudy again this morning, but as we left site at 8.00 am the cloud was starting to lift. We drove to Cocklawfoot and went by taxi to Byrness – a long journey round the Cheviot Hills passing Jedburgh at around the half way point. As we approached Byrness it was raining quite hard, but had eased once we started walking. However, the ground was damp, and the bracken and other foliage on the steep path up Byrness Hill got us wet for the first time this section.

A 'welcoming sign' on the moorland near Byrness!!?

It was a long steep climb up to the moorland above Byrness, and the weather had closed in so we didn't get views for a while, just moorland grasses and mist. Generally we were on moorland up and over undulating ground for most of the day. After about an hour or so the views gradually opened up and we could see vast stretches of moorland hills for miles, and it was this terrain that

Sign at the Roman Camp at Chew Green

Checking the map at Chew Green

made up the days walking. After about 5 miles we reached the ancient site of a Roman Camp and Medieval Village at Chew Green. From there we progressed to Lamb Hill, and our lunch stop.

Trig point at Lamb Hill

The views on our left became more interesting with views over the Scottish moors and further hills and fields. To our right were the green folds of moorland hillsides going on for ever.

In the main we were on the Scottish/English Border for most of the day: the ridge of the Pennine Way making a perfect natural border line.

The final and highest hill today was Windy Gyle, with 360 degree panoramic views at the summit and trig point.

We continued on from there to a cross-Pennine Path down a drovers road; Clennell Street; which took us down on a wide path for 2.5 miles back to our waiting car. We had walked just over 17 miles and it was 5.45 pm when we reached the car.

A decision was made to go to the pub in the village for a meal this evening, and after the usual refreshing shower and cup of tea we walked up to the pub and enjoyed a very good meal.

Day 62 Wednesday 24th July 2013 Cocklawfoot and Windy Gyle to Kirk Yetholm 15.0 miles

There had been some heavy rain in the night and we'd heard thunder rolling around last evening, so we were surprised to wake up to a lovely sunny morning. We were all ready by 8.00 am to be taken to Cocklawfoot (the site owner had kindly offered) and by 8.30 am we were walking up to a mile or so beyond Windy Gyle where we had left the Pennine Way yesterday. So we knew we were in for a long two and a half miles climb as we'd come down from there yesterday.

The scenery was lovely as we walked up and we made good time, reaching the Pennine Way in just on the hour. From here we were on flagstone paths through the boggy ground making good headway towards Kings Seat, and the views from the top were magnificent. Several large areas of cotton grass made it very pretty today, especially on the route up by Crookedsike Head and along to the turn off to the Cheviot. We had a short stop half way up here on a green grassy slope with a grand view spread out before and below us.

Up near the Cheviot turning we turned left up to Auchope Cairn, and on the way here the path was in the process of being relaid with stone. Previously it had been laid as a board walk over the boggy ground. We made our way up to the Cairn and this was the highest point of today's walk. The views were simply amazing, miles of countryside before us, patchwork of tiny fields in yellows and greens were far in the distance beyond the series of moorland hills and woodland. It was a lovely sunny day and we saw it at its best.

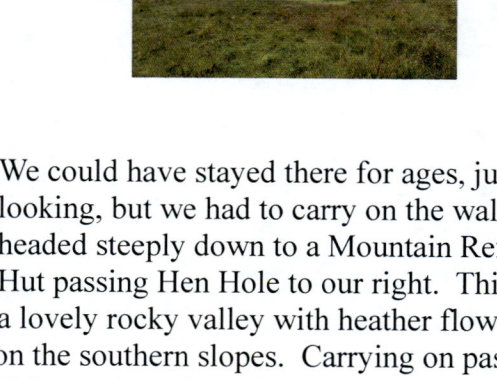

We could have stayed there for ages, just looking, but we had to carry on the walk and headed steeply down to a Mountain Refuge Hut passing Hen Hole to our right. This was a lovely rocky valley with heather flowering on the southern slopes. Carrying on past Hen Hole we passed another really pretty valley at Red Cribbs (red sandstone gully down to the green pastures below). On up to The Schil where we stopped for lunch and then we headed down from there round Black Hag. We decided to take the higher level Pennine Way Path, where there was a choice, and as we went up to White Law we were rewarded with a final sight of the magnificent views of the Scottish countryside before us before descending gradually to Halter Burn and then taking the lane up, *most definitely up*, and with views now to Kirk Yetholm.

On arrival at 'The End of The Pennine Way' at 'The Border' pub in Kirk Yetholm, we had to stop and have a drink – being as it was 'on the house' for those finishing the Pennine Way.

We all signed the Pennine Way visitor book and will be sent our Pennine Way Certificates in due course.

It was a very warm and sultry day as we descended to Town Yetholm and the skies behind us were darkening. We reached Town Yetholm and our caravans just before the thunderstorm hit. It rained heavily for quite a while, so much so that we had to drive to the pub for our celebration meal. The sun came out later and I was able to take this photo of the sun setting on our end of the Pennine Way.

Day 63   Monday 22ⁿᵈ July   Kirk Yetholm to Crailing (St Cuthbert's Way)   14.7 miles

(Andy took our car to Crailing and had a taxi back to site. As Bob's car is sick – and awaiting diagnosis as to how ill it is, we've decided to jump two sections of the walk – leaving the end of the Pennine Way until we've two cars available to leave at each end of the section.)

It was cloudy this morning, with rain in the air, as we left heading out of Town Yetholm to join St Cuthbert's Way. On fields at first and then to a wide track it was level walking.

Once we reached the lane it was a little more uphill and then we turned sharply right uphill on a track before heading up still further: on a path alongside fields of kale, carrying on for a couple more fields, still very much uphill, as we reached a ladder stile on to the hillside.

Still going uphill, to the top of Wideopen Hill, we enjoyed panoramic views all around – of the gentle landscape of the foothills below the Pennine Way. There were large arable fields; as far as could be cultivated on the hillsides; and quite a lot of woodland too.

In the far distance could be seen the three peaks of the Eildon Hills on St Cuthbert's Way, closer to Melrose: we shall pass these at some point in our walking.

From Wideopen Hill we went downhill and then uphill again to Grubbit Law above the village of Morebattle, with its two hill forts on the hills beyond.

Down to Morebattle crossing a footbridge at the bottom of the hill over a stream, and then we followed the lane downhill, passing a ford, and then up and over to Morebattle.

By this time it was just coming up to 12 noon and we hoped for refreshment at the pub. We were in luck, they opened a few minutes early for us and we enjoyed a drink and a chocolate bar before heading out on the road, passing very attractive hanging baskets and tubs along the wide main street.

On the road for quite a while and then on a smaller lane, where we found gooseberries, ripe and ready to pick, so we filled a couple of bags to take back before carrying on our walk through very pretty countryside until we reached Cessford Castle. This was a ruin at the top of the hill, with sheep grazing the castle grounds. There was a large tree giving shade which we welcomed as a lunchtime picnic spot, as the sun had come out and it was becoming a very hot and humid day.

From Cessford Castle we were on the lane and then a track past a row of farm cottages, passing vast fields of oats and barley, the barley was ripening in the sunshine so these fields were golden against the more blue-green of the oats.

We welcomed the sections of the path that went through, or past, shady woods, and we carried on in this way for several miles, with views all around. Then through fields downhill to a footbridge and up over crags before more quiet lane walking to a woodland section just before Crailing. A steep downhill on a lane took us down to Crailing and our waiting car.

Back at Town Yetholm, Lynne and I stopped off at the village shop to get supplies while Andy and Bob went back to site. Bob's car is still in the garage awaiting attention and we hoped they could have a hire car: but, sadly, not possible.

Day 64   Friday 26th July 2013   Crailing to Dryburgh Abbey   15.1 miles

A lovely sunny day, and not too hot, so very pleasant walking. The day's walk was a complete contrast to the end of the Pennine Way, but still very beautiful in a different, more gentle, way. Our path took us along Dere Street, an ancient Roman Road, and this was a good wide green lane at first before entering some woodland.

Our route took us toward the Monteviot Estate where the Roman Road was no longer in existence. The path was through shady woodland, with board walks and wooden bridges, and we detoured slightly to take advantage of refreshment at the Visitor Centre at Harestanes. Continuing back on St Cuthbert's Way through more woodland we eventually rejoined Dere Street, and now we were in more open countryside, with Dere Street a broad sweep of grassland ahead of us, with lovely mature beech trees and some oaks giving some welcome shade. Very pretty with much rosebay willowherb and other wild flowers to keep me busy taking photographs. We had Snailholm Tower in the Distance on the north side and ahead were the three peaks of the Eildon Hills toward Melrose. Behind us we could still see views across to the Pennines, so a most enjoyable walk. We passed Lady Lilliard's Grave: a feisty lady by all accounts who was very heroic in the Border Skirmishes; *'to the English gave many thumps and with legs cut off she fought on her stumps'!!!*

On towards the village of Maxton the route took us along a lane for a mile or so, and by this time we were looking for a spot in the shade to have our lunch. We found a pleasant spot in the churchyard behind Maxton Church. Continuing on St Cuthbert's Way the route took us down to the

River Tweed: a series of wooden steps down and then along a board walk to a wooden bridge across St Boswell's Burn and out to the banks of the River Tweed, where we were rewarded with breathtaking views up and downstream: a very pleasant spot.

Not far away up the bank was a well, and, above that, a most unusual 'donkey driven' water pump that in days past supplied a grand house. Also there was evidence of an ice house further along the riverside.

We walked along the River Tweed for several miles, at times high above the river on a well maintained path with a wooden handrail and, where necessary, wooden bridges and steps and board walks, Other sections were out in the open along the riverbank, and then alongside a riverside golf course (flapjack stop) and we continued in this very pleasant fashion until we reached the village of St Boswells, going uphill from the river past a very grand house / castle. After a 'cup of tea stop' in the village, recommended to us by some passing walkers, we continued along to the village green.

Bob and Lynne made enquiries about their car which was being repaired in the village, and then we continued our walk along the Tweed crossing at a road bridge, past a weir and old mill. Continuing on we reached the suspension bridge which we crossed to Dryburgh Abbey (and our waiting car). We called at the Abbey shop for ice creams before driving back to site. Over to Bob and Lynne's this evening for coffee and biscuits and planning the logistics of tomorrow's section. This was a fantastic day of walking, with magnificent views and great weather.

Day 65 Friday 27th July 2013 Dryburgh Abbey to Yair Bridge 15.1 miles

A day of two Scottish paths: Melrose was the end of St Cuthbert's Way and after Melrose we took the Southern Upland Way to Yair Bridge.

At Dryburgh we came across the Temple of Muses: just before we crossed the river on the suspension bridge. This was set up on the hillside and was a circular temple, with columns, in the middle of which were three sculpted life sized figures.

After a brief look there we crossed the river and carried on in woodland and on wooden walkways and similar paths to yesterday, along the beautiful River Tweed.

After a while St Cuthbert's Way left the river and we headed toward the Eildon Hills and the village of Bowden.

Once on the Eildon hills we were on a wide woodland path going uphill all the while until eventually we emerged from the tree line out on to heather clad hillside and could clearly see the brow of the hill between the larger two summits of the Eildon Hills.

From here was a grand view of Melrose and, further along the valley, the town of Galashiels, spread before us and set amidst the surrounding hills and woodlands. We were surprised how undulating, and beautiful, the countryside here was. High hills in all directions.

View of Melrose and Galashiels as we came down the Eildon Hills

View back to the Eildon Hills from Melrose Abbey

We walked down into Melrose and stopped for drinks at a cafe, before heading down to the river again, passing the Abbey on our right as we went. Very pretty alongside the river. The whole town of Melrose itself was beautifully kept with hanging baskets and beautiful flower beds in the town. Unfortunately a section alongside the river was spoilt by the litter that some thoughtless people had dropped, as it was such a lovely spot otherwise. Up along the riverside path we were high above the Tweed, and then we turned toward Galashiels Old Town, up and down hillsides and along a cycle route that was being turned back into a railway. We were back by the river again when we stopped for lunch in a small area of parkland (again spoilt by litter). When we reached the Old Town of Galashiels the Way took us though some parkland, with board walks, and then we were heading up toward Gala Hill.

Onwards, and up, out of the town across fields to a woodland and then an uphill path for quite a while. Eventually we reached the cairn at the top of the hill and started to descend the couple of miles to Yair Bridge over the River Tweed. The rain clouds were gathering and we hoped we were going to escape getting wet but about a mile before the end of the walk it rained very heavily and we had to stop and put waterproofs on. The rain was so heavy that we got quite wet doing so. Back to the car at Yair Bridge and we headed back to site.

Day 66   **Sunday 28th July 2013**   **Yair to Traquair**   **9.98 miles**

Heavy rain was forecast so we weren't surprised to hear the rain from 3 am onwards. We had already made the decision to see what the weather was like before making final plans for today's walking, and so we met together at around 10.30 am for coffee and decision making. It was forecast that the rain would clear in the afternoon and so we planned to leave site around 12 noon to drive to Traquair and then back to Yair to start the walk around 1.30 pm.

It was raining steadily, but not too heavy, as we started the walk from Yair Bridge along the lane to a forest track. The track went uphill for quite a distance, going through forest and then a more open valley with fir trees and masses of rosebay willowherb which made for very attractive views as we walked. On up through more forest, still going uphill, we were quite warm from the climb and stopped to take off waterproofs as the rain had begun to ease. Once out on in the open moorland we had to put them on again as the rain was a fine drizzle. Continuing up and over moorland and then more level walking for a while there were good views to be had as the cloud had begun to lift: the sun even tried to shine on us in places. Another uphill section brought us to the Three Brethren: a group of three cairns, and to a trig point, with excellent views all round.

Turning left from here on a stony track through heathery moorland we reached some grassy moorland, near a group of fir trees and stone wall, where we stopped for a very late lunch: it being 3.15 pm by then. After lunch we headed briefly downhill with the fir trees and stone wall on our left. Over a stile and the track ahead showed a definite, and very long, uphill section across heathery moorland. The top of this hill was the summit of Brown Knowe and once again there were some good views to be had right across to the Cheviots and the Pennine Way!

Down from here and passing forestry plantations of conifers: mist rising after the rain giving them an eerie and atmospheric feel. It was very pretty all along an ancient 800 year old drovers track known as Minchmoor Road. Along this route was 'Wallace's Ditch', where allegedly Wallace waited for his clans to assemble. Also we passed Cheese Well on this historic route, and were surprised to learn that Sir Walter Scott's daughter had travelled this ancient road in a coach and six horses: on her way to a Ball in Peebles; with six servants walking alongside ready to right the coach should it fall into a bog or ditch!! Our travelling today had no such problems despite the previous night's rain, and the path has been well maintained. Alongside the route was a sculpture, and beyond that the heather had been cut in circles. I took a photo through the hole in the sculpture.

On down to Traquair were the sounds of music festival in the distance. We had glorious views as we descended and the sun was finally winning its battle over the cloudy skies, giving a golden light to the valley below: the mist and rain in the distance over the River Tweed providing a real contrast. It was a great afternoon's walk and we were really pleased that we'd made the right decision in delaying the start of it today. We arrived at Traquair and our waiting car at just after 6 pm.

Back to Yair to collect Bob's car and then travel back to site. Lynne made a gooseberry crumble with the gooseberries we'd picked on our walk yesterday so we joined them for 'pudding' and a cup of tea this evening.

Day 67 **Monday 29th July 2013** **Traquair to White Meldon** **15.2 miles**

After parking our car at White Meldon: a remote and hilly area just north west of Peebles, we drove back in Bob's car to start our walk from Traquair. Today's walk was one of 'waterproofs on', then 'waterproofs off' as the weather was sunshine and showers: probably more of the latter!

To begin with we were on a lane heading toward Old Howford, before going left uphill on a track through Cardrona Forest plantation; mainly pine trees; and we were climbing for quite a while until we came out into the open at the top of Castle Knowe. From here we headed downhill through the forest and it was quite tricky navigating the path through this section. We had wanted to come out of the plantation on to Kailzie Hill and down into Peebles on the Old Drove Road, but even with the use of GPS for map references and Andy's map-reading skills, we were unable to find the route we needed. Instead we had to come down to Kirkburn and take the road for the remainder of the walk into Peebles.

Once in Peebles we headed for a lunch spot in Victoria Park. We found a seat (wet) by the river Tweed, and after spreading our orange groundsheet on the seat we were able to have our lunch. We were watched by an inquisitive raven and a couple of seagulls, who were anxiously waiting for a few crumbs!

It came on to rain quite hard and we made our way into the town via a lovely white bridge over the river, and headed for a tea shop.

Peebles is an interesting old town, and I especially liked the parish church, which is quite magnificent in its stonework and tower, and the town itself has many individual shops and some characterful buildings.

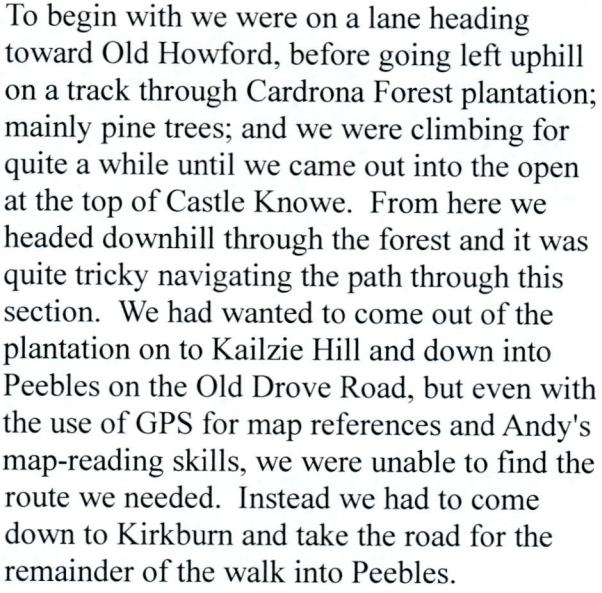

We headed out of the town towards the river Tweed and the gardens along the river bank were very pleasant with mature trees: many lime trees with their scent-laden blossom. As we walked beneath these we could hear the buzzing of many bees as they collected the nectar. At the end of the parkland was a pretty section of path that went over rocky ground up above the river and heading toward Neidpath Castle, where there was a short, steep climb up to the castle and the road.

Across the road next, and along towards the town for a short while, before heading up a track towards the hills and the golf course. Then uphill through woodland to come out to the moorland, and seeing a mast ahead. At this point the heavens opened and we quickly put on full waterproofs – there was hail and we could hear thunder rumbling around. However, below us, as we climbed there was an excellent view of the town of Peebles.

On across the moorland the path became unclear, although we were right according to the map and guide book. We made our way, but had to cross fences and closed gates and head uphill over heathery moor: quite difficult going from here, as we tried to get across to White Meldon Hill. Still no real path here and we ended up traversing the contours and then heading downhill, following sheep tracks through the heather and bracken to reach the bridge and stile at the bottom of the valley, and our waiting car. It was raining quite heavily across this section and so we were all pleased to reach the car and head back to Traquair, retrieve Bob's car and head back to site.

Day 68   Wednesday 31st July 2013   White Meldon to 3 miles after West Linton   12.1 miles

We parked at the foot of White Meldon: where we'd finished the walk on the day before yesterday. (We'd moved sites yesterday and are now staying near Carlops). Unlike yesterday, today there was a *clear* track on the ground, heading uphill through fir trees. Then one quite steep section up to a break in the trees before heading on a good track all the way to the top of the hill, and from there we were out on open moorland, with lovely views all around.

It was very quiet, there being no road access at all here, and we descended to a very pretty valley where we stopped to have a break. The valley was very green with a stream running along the bottom: Flemington Water, and there were large areas of rosebay willowherb here too.

The only occupants of the valley were sheep, and we saw one try and jump across the stream only to fall back in to the water, and then try again, nearly falling in, but just making it over and up the bank.

It was a lovely spot, but we couldn't stay there all day, so up on a good grassy path through bracken at times, and following the stream as we headed uphill to another stretch of woodland, coming out again to lovely views to the Pentland Hills and the village of Romannobridge.

We were on a drovers track which took us down to the village, and we had views towards our next destination: West Linton. Then two and a half miles of road walking to West Linton where we had our lunch on a bench overlooking the well kept green. Just behind us was the Old Toll Bridge Café, so we had tea and cakes before setting off again on through the village, and then uphill on a stony track to join a 'Roman Road' *(Agricola)*. Left then through a farm and out on to the hillside again to walk up a beautiful valley with Lyne Water down below us.

The steep sided valley and woodland made this a very attractive section as we headed uphill here, keeping the valley and stream on our left as we climbed. Then down to a footbridge across the stream and up a steep grassy bank the other side, up to the road and then along to our waiting car.

Day 69   **Friday 2ⁿᵈ August 2013**   **Wakefield to Lin's Mill Aqueduct**   **14.5 miles**

Andy and Bob took both cars and drove to Lin's Mill Aqueduct, bringing Bob's car back to collect Lynne and me: who for once had a leisurely morning doing the packed lunches. We set off to Wakefield, 3 miles beyond West Linton, where we had finished the previous section, and were walking by 9.50 am.

From Wakefield we were on a good track up to Baddinsgill Reservoir, with the Pentland Hills before us. After passing some Highland cattle and calf, we were out onto lovely heather clad moorland, and on a good path.

After a wet start, the weather was fine and sunny by now with a breeze behind us. Uphill and down dale for a while in remote and beautiful scenery to White Crags, we reached the viewpoint at Cauldstane Slap between East and West Cairn Hill. From here a view down to Harperigg Reservoir and a few houses and farms. A mile or so on we took the path round the steadings across a footbridge at Gala Ford and then we headed uphill again for about a mile to Little Vantage and the A70, which we crossed.

Crossing the marshy ground near the reservoir   *From Little Vantage: the view back towards the Pentland Hills before crossing the A70*

From here the uphill going was quite tough as there was no real path, just tussocky moorland grass and a few boggy sections to negotiate. As we continued uphill the wind became increasingly stronger making it difficult to stay upright at times. On we went until we reached the trig point at the top of Corston Hill. An excellent panorama was before us: we could see Edinburgh, the Firth of Forth and its railway bridge and, across to the west, towards Glasgow. It was extremely windy here and it stayed like that as we progressed down the ridge to a cairn.

From the cairn it was slightly better, as we were traversing the contours downhill, and we found a sheltered spot in the sunshine, out of the strong wind, to have our lunch.

Unfortunately, as we sat down for lunch Bob realised that his GPS was no longer with him. There was no option for him but to retrace his steps up the windy hillside to try and find it: it was a fair distance and back into the wind. After a while, Andy went to join him in the search: we'd seen Bob in the far distance by the cairn and then seen him carry on to the trig point. After a while they both returned and, quite amazingly, Bob had found it: it would appear that in the strong wind the velcro straps had been pulled apart. The GPS had dropped to the ground near the trig point where the wind was at its strongest. *Much relieved, Bob was then able to have his lunch!!*

After this incident we carried on, quite steeply down hill, across the rough grasses until we reached a track which led to a lane. We were on the lane for about a mile before crossing two railway bridges, and then further along the lane we reached the A71, which we crossed, taking a path into the Almondvale and Calder Wood Country Park. The path followed the River Almond, although the high and steep tree-covered banks made it impossible to see the river below.

The path took us through silver birch woodland: and many wild raspberries were to be had along the way. After a mile or so we found ourselves with a clearer view of the river as we reached the road bridge high above us at mid Calder. We left the Country Park here to take a detour into Mid Calder and have cold drinks at The Black Bull pub: we were quite amused to see three television screens here, all on, so you could have sight of one wherever you were sat. After this refreshing stop, we went back into the Country Park to continue our route which took us along the river.

We made a mistake here, taking a wrong path which led to a very steep incline; muddy too; up from the river. Andy went up and made it to the top. Bob, Lynne and I tried to follow.

After we'd taken a few difficult steps up this incline, Andy had noticed the correct path and suggested we retrace our steps. However, once Bob and Lynne had set themselves to the task of climbing this incline there was no stopping them: although I don't think Lynne was so keen on the idea. I decided to retrace my steps back to the bridge and found the path we should have taken. Hoping that I would find the others I set off in what I hoped was the right direction. Not long afterwards I came across them, Bob and Lynne just about making it to the top of the incline as I arrived. Carrying on now, on the much better path, we continued along the hillside above the River Almond.

At one point some of the water was diverted into a leat and we followed this right back to the canal at Lin's Mill Aqueduct, about three miles away: sometimes it was visible next to the path and at other times it was in tunnels under the hillside. As we neared the Union Canal we came out into the open and a beautiful pastoral scene was before us: Lin's Mill Aqueduct high above and the river far

below finding its way through the sheep grazed pasture land. A short distance further on, as we reached the track to the car park, the 'leat' went into a tunnel: appearing again as we approached the car park and canal.

Day 70 Thursday 1st August 2013 Lin's Mill Aqueduct to Linlithgow 13.1 miles

It was quite a journey round the Edinburgh ring road and then M8 and M9, to park at the canal at Linlithgow. Then back in Bob's car to start walking at Lin's Mill Aqueduct: which was very impressive. We followed the Union Canal between Edinburgh and Glasgow today, so it was level walking and a good path, albeit with some puddles from the overnight and morning's rainfall.

The raindrops on the tall grasses were very pretty and worthy of a photo or two. The rain: soon it eased. We took off waterproofs and from then on it was mostly fine, just a little rain now and again, so much better than forecast.

To begin with we were under the flight path to Edinburgh airport, with planes passing overhead every few minutes, and then a little later on we were passing 'slag heaps' from an industrial past, some now grown over with grass and shrubs and others quite bare. One was just behind a very nice old castle and it seemed a shame that the view from the castle had disappeared. Along the canal were many wild flowers to look at and also the different bridges. There wasn't much in boat traffic today – only one passed us as we walked. We broke our tow path walk at Broxburn, where we headed into the town and managed to find a good coffee stop (complete with bacon butties) before rejoining the towpath a little further on. Through a canal cutting for quite a while with trees either side which, although pretty, meant not much variation in view. However we came out of this section into more open countryside and after a few miles stopped to have our lunch at a picnic table near a canal bridge.

We weren't far from Linlithgow now and soon arrived back at the car. We decided: having seen an advertisement for a tea room half a mile or so further on, to walk along to the tea room and explore the town. We were very glad we did, as the Linlithgow Palace (ruin) and St Michael's Church was well worth the visit, and we learned that this was the birthplace of Mary Queen of Scots. It was in a magnificent setting above the Loch and an interesting building altogether. We also looked at transport links between Falkirk Wheel and Linlithgow for Saturday's final part of this section of LeJog.

Day 71 Saturday 3rd August 2013 Linlithgow to the Falkirk Wheel 12.6 miles

Today was an early start, as Bob's car was now repaired and ready to collect, but to do that we had to drive back to St Boswells, so we left at 7.30 am to arrive at the garage for 8.30 am. It took a little while to get everything sorted – paperwork etc., but soon we were on our way to Linlithgow to start the last section of this year's walk. We parked near the station and decided that we needed a hot drink before we set off, and found a café in the town.

Suitably revived we headed off along the towpath of the Union Canal once more, heading for the Falkirk Wheel about twelve miles away.

Whether it was the late start and the feeling that we needed to make up for lost time, or merely that the end of the section was in sight, the men set a fast pace the whole day: on a mission to succeed! Lynne and I managed to keep up and we set a pace of 3.4 mph for quite a time. Lunch was had on a grassy bank along the canal and off we set again – we were all keen to get to the tunnel, towards the end of the walk, which was about half a mile long. It was lit so we didn't need our torches and we could see where the tunnel was man made, and where it was carved through the natural rock.

After this we kept up the pace as we headed for the Falkirk Wheel, passing mile posts every so often: giving distances to Edinburgh and the Falkirk end of the Union Canal, so we could keep a check on our progress.

At the end of the mileposts, there was a newer section of canal: a further two canal locks and a modern tunnel under the Roman Antonine Wall that had been specially constructed to connect to the Falkirk Wheel on the Forth and Clyde Canal. From the new tunnel we had sight of five semi-circular arches above the canal and, ahead, the top section of the Falkirk Wheel. The canal appeared to stop 25 metres above the ground at the point where it reached the Wheel – a canal suspended in mid-air. Beyond that, far in the distance were the Trossach Hills: so quite a view.

We walked alongside the canal as far as we were able, and took photographs of the Wheel turning and a boat arriving at the Upper level of canal. It is an amazing piece of engineering and we took the path down to the lower level: the canal basin of the Forth and Clyde Canal, and sat on the grass to watch two boats going up and two boats coming down: the caissons revolving on giant cogs to reach the relevant canal level.

The Falkirk Wheel is vast and spectacular, so this was an excellent place for the ending of this year's walk section.

We have now walked 248 miles this year and a total of 985 miles since Land's End, so it was fitting that we took ourselves off to the Allan Ramsey Hotel in Carlops for a meal when we got back to site. It was an excellent meal in a comfortable 18th Century Hotel, and so we ended this year's walking in style!

Andy, Meg, Bob and Lynne at the Falkirk Wheel

Next year – two days walk to the start of the West Highland Way and then we will take the East Highland Way to Aviemore.

Day 72 Sunday May 11th 2014 Falkirk Wheel to Kirkintilloch 15 miles

We arrived at the Falkirk Wheel, leaving Bob's car there: ours was already parked at Kirkintilloch, and had a photo stop where we had finished the walk last year. There were now two small scale sculptures of the 'Kelpies', which are two large horse heads: the final, and much larger, sculptures are a distance away, and not seen by us. We took a couple of photos of the four of us before setting off along the Forth and Clyde Canal. Unfortunately we were too early to see the Falkirk Wheel in action this morning as it didn't open until 10 am.

At the Falkirk wheel for the start of this year's section of LeJog

Reflections on the Forth & Clyde Canal

Our walk followed the Forth and Clyde Canal all day today, and it was very pretty, and far more 'open' than the last section along the Union Canal. There were views to the Kilsyth Hills on our right and the whole walk was very 'green' with the new leaves out on the trees all around. The reflections in the canal were stunning in the sunlight. It was a very good path and there were many people out on bikes, or walking or jogging: today being a Sunday. We saw swans nesting, a couple of herons and heard much birdsong as we walked.

In true 'LeJog' fashion the first promised port of call for a coffee stop wasn't available: although there was a sign on the lock that there was 'food all day'. This was a complete fallacy, as when we arrived at the lock the nearby pub had been badly burnt by a fire!! So no coffee stop after all.

No chance of refreshments here!

However, we were used to this kind of setback by now: how many coffee shops have we arrived at and found closed since we started from Land's End? We stopped a while further on by another lock to have our flasks of coffee, sat in the sunshine – all very pleasant.

Glimpses of the Antonine Roman Wall as we walked today. With bluebells and many wild flowers along the path it was pleasant walking. In the spring sunshine one of the lock gate keepers was 'hard at work' lying down along the arm of the lock gate.

The canal was very wide for much of the way – looking more like a river here than a canal at first glance. One section of the river was straight for two miles, and then we came across a meandering section which was tree-lined and the path bordered by cow parsley in flower.

Just before we reached Kirkintilloch, about a mile or so to go, we celebrated that we'd reached 1,000 miles since Land's End (a legendary flapjack stop and a photo sufficed) and then we continued back to the car at Kirkintilloch. This is the last of the canal walking. Tomorrow we head towards Milngavie (pronounced 'Mull-guy') along a disused railway line.

Back at site it rained for most of the evening. The forecast for tomorrow is dry mainly, but showers developing in the afternoon. Today's forecast had been showers, some heavy, but we started out in sunshine, and we managed the whole walk without getting wet: it just started raining as we were getting into our car on reaching Kirkintilloch. So we were fortunate today as there were some prolonged heavy showers around.

Day 73   **Monday 12th May 2014**   **Kirkintilloch to Milngavie**   **9.5 miles**

We left our car at Kirkintilloch and then set out along the disused Strathblane Railway. Alongside the river; Glazert Water; this was another pleasant walk on a good tarmac surface. Many walkers and cyclists again at the start. Going past Milton of Campsie we continued on toward Lennoxtown, where we came off the railway path.

There was a sign to a hotel, which we decided to investigate for a coffee stop: we were in luck – it was open and we sat outside and had coffee, hot chocolate, tea, cappuccino, respectively. Deciding it was a good place to eat, we decided to book a meal there this evening to celebrate properly our achievement of 1,000 miles since Land's End. Walking on from there we were heading uphill on a track away from Lennoxtown: our first real uphill this section of LeJog. We were rewarded with fine views back as we climbed up to Forestry Commission land, passing Glen Whapple along the way, where Bob and Lynne had a photo taken. *There are many 'Pikes' on the maps (our surname), so Bob and Lynne (Whapples) were pleased to find somewhere named after them for a change!*

Bob & Lynne at Glen Whapple

145

It was pleasant going through woodland, although many trees had been blown down in previous gales and were across the path at one point: we could easily have followed a different and more obvious track. Fortunately Andy, and Dexter, had their wits about them and we ended up on the right route. The fir trees were just getting their pine cones, which were red, and there was new spring green colour at the tips of the branches.

Our new dog 'Dexter', just 6 months old, bounds towards me and the camera

Views to the tower blocks of the city of Glasgow: glimpsed between the gorse bushes

Coming out of the woodland across the hillside there were some streams to cross. Much gorse flowering up here, with views from this high point across to the urban sprawl and high rise buildings of Glasgow. Out on to a narrow lane, where Dexter was very excited by the young bullocks who kept up with us as we walked past their field: eventually giving up following us as we went further uphill. We had good views all the way, still towards Glasgow, and in the far distance a range of hills which looked like the Pentland Hills in shape: and which, if that was correct, were now four days walk behind us. A little further on we had our first view of the reservoir north of Milngavie, and shortly afterwards we arrived at a road junction: some beautiful rhododendrons and azaleas by a cottage here.

Taking a lane towards the caravan site, and after crossing two fields, we were back. We still hadn't had lunch, deciding to press on while the weather was good. There were downpours of rain around, but we were fortunate in escaping these. We had our lunch back at site just after 1 pm. After lunch we walked into Milngavie to get food supplies. We stopped at the Information Centre, which was principally concerned with promoting the town being the start of the West Highland Way, and found that we can get our LeJog forms stamped with the West Highland Way logo tomorrow morning before we set off. This evening we drove to the Glazert Country House Hotel, where we'd had coffee earlier, and had a very nice evening meal. So we're all set for the West Highland Way tomorrow– the forecast is dry and sunny, with some cloud, so hopefully we'll have some good views.

Day 74 **Tuesday 13th May 2014** **Milngavie to Drymen** **15.5 miles**
(First section of the West Highland Way.)

Andy and Bob set off at 8 am to leave our car at Drymen. Meanwhile Lynne and I prepared packed lunches in readiness. We set off walking down to Milngavie, via the two reservoirs. Our first stop was the West Highland Way Information Centre where we had our LeJog forms stamped with the West Highland Way logo, and our photo taken at the start.

The start of the West Highland Way

Uphill in Mugdock Wood

We set off through Mugdock Wood and Country Park where there were bluebells among the very new green grass and trees. There was a diversion of the West Highland Way at one point which gave us an extra mile to walk: however it did mean we were on higher ground and had great views back over the valley and across to the Pentland Hills behind us and to mountain ranges ahead of us. Coming out through woodland and onto more open ground we arrived at Mugdock Castle, and a little further on were the views I've already mentioned. We stopped for a coffee break, sitting on a bank, admiring the scene before us. A little further on was an old gun-site.

Bluebells in Mugdock Country Park

Mugdock Castle

From there we went through woodland, generally downhill, to a road where we rejoined the original route. Then off to the right, away from the road, on a track uphill. On reaching the top we had more fantastic scenery as we were now out in the open and heading down hill to Dumgoyach: a tree covered conical shaped hill amongst the open moorland. Very scenic.

Approaching Dumgoyach

Once past the hill the path took us on a disused railway for several miles, a water pipeline alongside it taking water to Glasgow from Loch Lomond. Very open countryside both sides. Part way along the old railway we arrived at Beech House café and bar, where we sat at picnic tables to have our sandwiches. The weather was really kind today: some cloud, but sunny and dry, so it was very pleasant sitting having our lunch in those conditions. We continued on along the old railway, passing a garden centre, and having the main road not far away from us along this section.

Eventually we left the railway path and were on very pretty lanes to Gartness, where there was a bridge and a waterfall. There was a row of cottages here, the first of which had a fridge freezer outside with ice creams, drinks and chocolate bars for sale: via an honesty box. Sat on a nearby wall, and in the sunshine, we enjoyed our ice creams and chocolate bars before heading on along very pretty countryside, the lanes edged with bluebells, and with views across the fields down to a river. Still with the mountains ahead of us, the lane climbed steeply in places and we continued in this manner until we reached the outskirts of Drymen, where the path took us across a large cow field and then to another road into Drymen.

Lane after Gartness

Day 75   **Wednesday 14th May 2014**   **Drymen to Rowardennan**   **15 miles**

The weather was kind again today and we awoke to blue skies. We set off at 8 am to take our car to Rowardennan and Bob's car to the start of the walk from Drymen. Heading out of Drymen we took an uphill path to Queen Elizabeth Forest Park and on towards Conic Hill. The path took us through flowering gorse and broom up to an area of deforested land, with good views of Loch Lomond. The birdsong here was lovely: many willow or wood warblers to entertain us as we walked. In a pool there were young tadpoles. Dexter was able to be off the lead and had fun running back and forth fetching sticks. We passed many new timber stacks along our way.

We eventually reached the point of this section which is closed between 14th April and 14th May, inclusive, and *always* closed to dog walkers, so we had to take the lower, alternative, route which meant some road walking to Balmaha, but it was still very pleasant and we had good views of Conic Hill as we descended to the road at Milton of Buchanan. A mass of wild garlic flowering in the foreground of our view of Conic Hill was another photo I just *had* to take. As we reached the road we turned right and there were some beautiful gardens with flowering, and very colourful, azaleas and rhododendrons. On reaching Balmaha we stopped for coffee break / ice creams before heading up Craigie Fort.

The harbour at Balmaha

The path to Craigie Fort

The path up to Craigie Fort was very steep, but also very, very beautiful with bluebells covering the slopes amidst some trees: added to this were the views over Loch Lomond. So many photos were taken here. The view from the top was simply stunning! From there it was a pretty walk downhill, more bluebells and also primroses, wood anemone and violets to add to the scene.

Lynne at the viewpoint at Craigie Fort

Dexter's first swim was here

A little further on we had some beach walking and Dexter enjoyed fetching sticks thrown into the water, and even ended up having his first ever swim. He was much intrigued by the waves rippling ashore! After this we were heading inland to the road, and the path took us quite close by on a track through more woodland.

(This wasn't my finest hour, as I tripped and fell bruising my hand and worst of all, splitting my lip and dislodging what I thought were two teeth. It turned out later to be my 'bridged' tooth pushing up into the gum and coming adrift. I didn't find this out until we finished the walk and we luckily managed to see a dentist in Drymen – they were brilliant – I couldn't have asked for better service – and my tooth can be re-cemented in tomorrow at 6 pm. Much better outcome than I'd feared!!!!!)

Once I'd recovered from falling, cleaning myself up took a while: a nearby stream was helpful, although it was the stone over this very small stream that had sent me flying in the first place. We then continued on through the woodland to later cross the road, where we had a lunch stop, or rather Lynne, Bob and Andy had lunch – I could only manage a drink at that point.

We continued through more woodland with views of Ben Lomond, and occasional lakeside views, as we made our way over the last 5 miles or so to Rowardennan.

It was a very beautiful walk today: 15 miles covered. So far this section we've done 15 miles on day one, 9 miles on day two, 16 miles yesterday and 15 today – a total of 55 miles.

Day 76   Thursday 15th May 2014   Rowardennan to Invernarnan   14.5 miles

We started walking at 9 am from Rowardennan, in lovely sunny weather: a few clouds around, but nothing to worry about. The route followed a good track uphill and then along a wide track for several miles, with views of the loch between the trees and with waterfalls cascading into the loch from our right.

Bluebells on the banks of Loch Lomond

One of the many waterfalls on the upper slopes

It was all very pretty, and good walking too, and we made reasonable time: only stopping at a viewpoint with a seat about an hour or so later to have a coffee break. Carrying on from there, still on the wide high level track: as the low level track was undergoing improvements and wasn't open. Passing bluebell woods and waterfalls, we continued until the track went downhill and re-joined the low level route to Inversnaid. The path was more interesting now, being narrower and winding through woodland or open meadow all carpeted with bluebells.

Carpets of bluebells; Loch Lomond

Waterfall at Inversnaid

On arriving at Inversnaid there was an impressive wide waterfall which we crossed by two bridges to reach the path past the hotel and on up the loch. Here the path was much more difficult in places with boulders and crags to negotiate. One boulder, situated close to a large tree, only had just enough room to squeeze by; difficult with a large rucksack; and another rock face had to be ascended by ladder, making for much slower progress now.

Negotiating the rocky shoreline

Just enough room to squeeze through here

This was compensated for by the very beautiful surroundings and also the many species of wild flowers: primroses, violets, celandine, greater stitchwort, trefoil, birds-eye, wood anemone and, of course, the bluebells.

Our very scenic lunch spot today

Added to this we had the cuckoo making his presence known much of the day. As we reached the end of the difficult section, which was about four miles, the path went away from the loch through quite different countryside: lush green grass and reeds and the occasional splash of bright yellow of the marsh marigolds.

Round Creag a Mhadaidh and then back to the loch side for a while to reach the end of the loch, passing a derelict cottage, picturesque in its location above the loch and with the mountains all around.

Derelict cottage at the end of Loch Lomond

From here the path took us up and round, skirting the sides of Cnap Mor on grassy fellside, then continued though woodland to eventually descend to a campsite.

Path around Cnap Mor as we leave Loch Lomond

A path from there over the river took us to our waiting car at Inverarnan. We decided on a good meal tonight, at the Glazert Hotel again, as it was quite late after we'd collected our car from Rowardennan *(and I'd visited the dentist at Drymen in the meantime to have my tooth re-fixed)*.

Day 77 **Saturday 17th May 2014** **Invernarnan to Tyndrum** **13.5 miles**

After overnight rain, it was a very different outlook this morning. Gone was the view of the mountains with snow on, and instead we had misty fine rain and clouds covering the tops. When we arrived at Tyndrum yesterday, on our 'move site day', the views were absolutely spectacular as it was a bright and clear sunny day. *I really should have taken a photo then.* However, we reluctantly resigned ourselves to the fact that the weather had changed and in wet weather gear we set off from Inverarnon, where we left the car, to walk to Tyndrum.

Being alongside the River Falloch and the Falloch Falls, today was a walk of waterfalls (and water falling). It was a pleasant walk on a good track along the River Falloch, going uphill much of the way and admiring the many waterfalls that we passed. It was very busy along the route with many walkers. The rain hadn't entirely closed off the views, but the tops were in cloud all day, which was a shame. After the river section we headed uphill to cross under the railway through 'Sheep Creep', which was a tunnel high enough for the sheep but a challenge for us taller walkers with rucksacks.

From the railway we headed mainly uphill on another good track, passing a farm: Keilator, in the valley to our right and with some good hills beyond. We then entered woodland, mainly pine trees, and the route took us up and down many hills through here, reaching a viewpoint as we left Glen Falloch behind, and entered Strath Fillan with the River Fillan meandering through the valley below us. There was more woodland for a couple of miles and we stopped to have lunch sat on a few logs by the side of the path: we were all quite hungry by then, as we'd walked 9 miles.

Carrying on through the woodland we came out to cross the A82 heading to Kirkton Farm and the remains of St Fillan's church. On another good track across the fells to Auchtertyre and then back to go under the A82. Alongside the river now, and then up over open ground before entering more woodland (Tyndrum Community Forest) on our approach to Tyndrum, and following the River Fillan all the way back to site.

Day 78   Monday 19th May 2014   Tyndrum to Forest Lodge   10.5 miles

Yesterday was wet all day, and it had been raining since the evening of the 16th May. We made the decision to wait until today to walk to Forest Lodge, via the Bridge of Orchy, as we had been told that this was one of the most scenic sections of the West Highland Way.

So yesterday was spent on site and in catching up on chores: washing and the like, and more pleasurable pursuits such as music making with Bob and Lynne, and then a game of Rummikub in the evening.

We were rewarded by our wait, as today was blue skies and sunshine for the most part, and our route down the valley, passing Ben Odhar with its distinctive conical shape, was very pleasurable: a good path along the old military road and some of the best scenery so far, only marred slightly by traffic noise from the A82 and the occasional train on the line to Fort William as each route fought for space in the narrow part of the valley.

There were some magnificent mountains in all directions, some still snow covered despite the recent rainfall. The path took us past Ben Dorain, crossing the railway occasionally, eventually crossing a river on a military road bridge.

Had a short drink stop, and took a photo of the four of us along this section, before heading off to the Bridge of Orchy: another military road bridge but much more grand! We stopped at the Bridge of Orchy Hotel to have coffee / hot chocolate, before taking an uphill track over the mountainside, at first though woodland and then on the open moorland, where we were rewarded with a superb view (360 degrees) down to Loch Tulla and across to the Glencoe Range of mountains and the bleak Rannoch Moor: which we shall cross on tomorrow's walk. Today we carried on along the track to reach a lonely rowan tree, the only deciduous tree in sight, and we stopped here at this view-point to have our lunch, before descending to Inveroran. The views today were fantastic and we were right to wait to walk this section – well worth it. On to near Forest Lodge and our waiting car.

Day 79   **Tuesday 20th May 2014**   **Forest Lodge to Altnafeadh**   **13 miles**

We drove to Altnafeadh to leave our car: and this was a spectacular drive over Rannoch Moor on the A82, the clouds were lifting from the mountains and there was an ethereal quality to it all. Having left our car, we travelled in Bob's car over the moor to Victoria Bridge car park, near Forest Lodge, just past Inveroran where we'd finished walking yesterday. From the car park the route took us over Victoria Bridge, with good views along Loch Tulla, and then uphill behind a plantation of pine trees for a while. Steadily climbing and on a really good track – the original A82 designed by Telford – now a good stony path.

We continued uphill and then the view opened out into the empty wilderness that is Rannoch Moor, its vast mountains around the moor in a 360 degree vista. Today there was snow on the tops, one patch of snow was shaped like a butterfly. Rannoch Moor is incredibly beautiful in its bleakness and remoteness, with many small lakes breaking up the view, and groups of silver birches on the tiny islands in these lakes. With the grandeur of the mountains around us and with good weather we had the best of it all and made good progress over the moor, the panorama before us mostly too vast to put in one photograph – it just wouldn't do it justice. However, we did our best and the views were indeed breathtaking.

We crossed a wide stream at Ba Bridge and, still mainly heading uphill, we made our way up over to Glen Etive, with the distant Grampian Mountains beyond.

As we came over into this new panorama we could see it was dominated by Buachaille Etive Mor, a very steep sided mountain described in our guide book as being one of Britain's most beautiful and shapely mountains (shown in the photograph: below left).

Our track now went downhill to the ski lift centre at Glencoe: we diverted a little here to take advantage of the café, and enjoy a bacon butty, as it was nearing lunchtime. From here we continued down to Blackrock Cottage which was once a climbing hut run by the Ladies' Scottish Climbing Club. Crossing the A82 at this point, we were now at the head of Glen Etive and Glencoe, and the surrounding awe-inspiring mountains.

We carried on to King's House Hotel where we stopped nearby for the rest of our lunch. There were deer here, fed on left-overs: courtesy of the hotel owners! We continued on towards Glencoe, uphill from the A82 for a while on another pretty path, and then descended to Altnafeadh and our waiting car. It had been a fine day's walking and the weather held, only clouding up and giving a little rain as we drove back to retrieve Bob's car from Victoria Car Park.

Day 80   **Wednesday 21st May 2014**   **Altnafeadh to Kinlochleven**   **6.5 miles**

It was quite a long drive this morning to leave our car at Kinlochleven, but as the forecast was only good from 10am we didn't leave Tyndrum until 8.30 am. As we drove down Glencoe it was a foreboding scene with the dark clouds clinging to the mountain sides. As we reached Kinlochleven the skies were still very cloudy. On returning to Altnafeadh it was beginning to brighten, and we started walking at 9.45 am. The path left Glencoe and rose via a mainly zigzag stony path, known as the Devil's Staircase, alongside a stream to begin with.

It was a stony track and not overly steep: but was relentless in its ascent. There were good views to be had behind us as we climbed: back to the snow on the high peaks around Glencoe.

As we reached the summit of our climb there was bare moorland ahead of us, which went downhill to start with but then ascended to a grand view of Blackwater reservoir and the mountains around.

This was the highest point on the West Highland Way.

The clouds were beginning to lift ahead of us and the sun came out more frequently as we made the

long descent down to Kinlochleven, at first down a stony track which frequently resembled a small stream, and then, once down to the large pipes carrying the water down to Kinlochleven for hydro-electric power, we were on a wide track downhill through silver birch trees. We passed a couple of good waterfalls as we reached Kinlochleven, and saw where the hydro-electric power station discharged the water from the large pipes back into the river and so into Lochleven.

We arrived at Kinlochleven shortly after 1.30 pm and drove back to Glencoe to collect Bob's car and return to Tyndrum. We'd made the decision to move on today after all, and packed up and moved after a late lunch. This was so we could take advantage of the better walking weather tomorrow, rather than spend the day moving site and shopping for food. It's a strenuous 14 miles tomorrow. On arrival at Glen Nevis site we set up camp and then walked into Fort William, which is at the end of the West Highland Way. We later had a meal at The Crofter Pub in the town.

Day 81   Thursday 22nd May 2014   Kinlochleven to Fort William   14.5 miles

After parking Bob's car at Kinlochleven, the route took us along the road for a short while before turning right opposite the school and going through woodland. Crossed a couple of streams, after which the path ascended by rough stone steps and carried on uphill to reach open ground and to a grand view over Kinlochleven. By this time we'd climbed the same height as the Devil's Staircase on the previous day, but this seemed harder going.

After a while the track joined a wider stony track and we were now in different countryside: the route could be seen a long way ahead as it followed the length of the glen. It was quite remote up here: a hard life for the previous occupants of the now ruined farm dwelling that we passed, and this was a long section of several miles of moorland.

It was busy today with several groups of West Highland Way walkers in the distance as they made their way, like ants, up hill and down dale towards the end of the glen before turning to head northwards. From here it was a previously wooded section, now cut down, providing us with a choice of tree stumps to sit on for lunch.

After a while the scenery changed as the route took us on a smaller track up on to a grassy hill, carrying on along this hillside to a group of fir trees. The path undulated through this woodland and this was a very pretty section.

163

Eventually down to cross a stream, and then up through more woodland, with the occasional view of Ben Nevis. A challenging ascent of the next hillside before coming down into more woodland on the slopes near Fort William.

Out on a forest track for a while, and with an extra diversion of a winding path down through trees, we eventually reached the point where the path left the forest track and headed between fields across to the Glen Nevis Road. As our site was close by, we stopped there for a cup of tea before going down to the town to have our photo taken at the official end of the West Highland Way, and to have our LeJog forms stamped with the Fort William logo for this end of the West Highland Way.

That done, Andy and Bob went to retrieve Bob's car from Kinlochleven, while Lynne and I cooked a meal, ready for the men's return.

Day 82   Friday 22nd May 2014   Fort William to Spean Bridge   12 miles
(First section of the East Highland Way)

We left Fort William at 9.30 am, having taken one car to Spean Bridge. The way at first went through the town until we reached the hydro-electic power station and the aluminium smelting plant. Here we took a right turn off the busy main road and headed up on a rough track past the plant, and were soon on a smaller track through woodland, mainly birch trees, and broom which was in flower and very attractive here. We followed this until we crossed a footbridge, where we had a coffee stop – a few midges around so we didn't linger too long.

On for a while before crossing a deep gorge by a footbridge. We then headed downhill past the golf course, and then the car park: for walkers and climbers attempting to climb Ben Nevis from the North Face. After crossing a minor road we were then on a path into Lochaber Forest and, later on, into Leanachan Forest. After this we were on an old military road crossing farmland, complete with two Highland Cattle, and into another field where, whilst walking uphill for a while, we found a lovely picnic spot with views of Ben Nevis to one side and the railway below us.

We had hoped to see the steam train go by, but were unlucky. Heading through the farm we then turned right uphill on a small lane, and then on a stony track. Here, as there had been along the way today, was gorse and broom flowering, which made a lovely foreground to the mountain scenery around us.

Into the forest again on a wide track which continued past a large pond, and then downhill. We eventually reached a smaller path which took us down to Spean Bridge station.

We stopped in Spean Bridge, by the Mill Gift Shop, to have the inevitable cup of tea, before returning to site.

Day 83   Saturday 24th May 2014   Spean Bridge to Inverlair – East Highland Way   10 miles

We left Spean Bridge walking generally uphill on a lane. Many silver birch trees around, and across the meadows were views across to the snowy topped mountains in the distance. Our first glimpse, this year, of cotton grass growing here.

Waymarker post for the East Highland Way

We continued on the lane, which eventually became a track after we crossed a stream near the Insh Scout Campsite. The track continued uphill, still near the river Spean for a while, and then the way took us through farmland, passing a recently harrowed field. It was just at this point that we saw the first East Highland Way Marker of the walk so far. We walked through pastoral grassland and then entered oak woodland, still near the river Spean. This was very pretty in the sunshine which we were fortunate to have today.

We stopped at the top of a rise in the track in a more open area, and sat on a fallen tree trunk to have coffee. On through more oak tree woodland, on a wide track, the path winding as it negotiated the streams that cascaded into the river below: one timber bridge over a waterfall was marked '*light vehicles only*'. The track continued across green pasture land with deciduous trees, and with good views to the higher mountains around us.

We descended to Monessie Farm, passing many young lambs here, and took a diversion to see the impressive suspension bridge over Monessie Falls: only *'two persons at a time'* could cross, and it still bounced and swayed as we crossed it. The gorge below was deep and spectacular, and worth the diversion.

On from Monessie Farm across more pasture land alongside the river: sheep grazing. We headed for a ruined croft, Achnacochine ruins, and sat here to have our lunch. A short while after this we had to cross the Allt nam Bruach ford before heading uphill on a forest track for a while. Descending, at a radio mast, into the hamlet of Inverlair, we took a lane to a metal bridge across a very deep and impressive gorge, before crossing the railway bridge and reaching our car.

Trying not to get wet feet here at the ford

The impressive gorge passed on our way back to the car after Inverlair

Day 84   **Sunday 25th May 2014**   **Inverlair to Moy Bridge**   **10 miles**

It was raining this morning when we woke, and it looked as though it was here to stay, but the weather broke a little and it dried up as we started walking from Inverlair to Fersit. The way took us up a lane, very pretty through wooded moorland after crossing some open moorland to begin with. The lane wound its way uphill for a while until we reached An Dubh Lochan (small inky black lake) where there was a 500 year old millstone that used to belong to the 2nd Chief of Koppach.

On to the hamlet of Fersit on the lane at first and then crossing a stream on Fersit Bridge (where Dexter managed to fall down off of a grassy ledge to the bank of the waters below). Also crossed the railway line here.

The hamlet of Fersit was pretty and once through the hamlet we came onto more open moorland. The cloud was hugging the sides of the mountainsides for most of the day, and so we couldn't see the tops, but it was still a good view. With the track veering round to our left we carried on past a stream and then entered Corrour Forest. The guide book stated that it was a 6 mile walk on forest tracks which sounded a little monotonous, but it was much better than we anticipated, with views occasionally through the deforested sections, and trees other than firs giving some variety.

There was some interest on the way: a small dam by a pretty stream and waterfall was good

for a photo or two. We stopped for coffee break, finding some tree trunks to sit on, and there was a bit of a view here through the trees.

169

Carrying on after coffee we passed the track to the Moy Reservoir Dam. This wasn't our route but we decided to take a diversion to look at the dam: it was about a third of a mile away. To our disappointment the dam couldn't be seen through the trees, and although we were very near, it was fenced off for safety reasons. (We decided to stop and look at it on our way back to site in the car, and get photos then.)

A lunch stop next with a view of Moy Reservoir: due to some de-forestation, and we were lucky to stay dry. There was much grey cloud around, with only a little blue sky here and there. Carrying on after lunch above the reservoir on

forest tracks until we eventually descended to Moy Bridge. Crossing the bridge over the river we arrived back at our cars. There were lupins flowering alongside broom here which was very pretty.

Back to site, via the supermarket in Fort William to get supplies, hoping to pack up the awning ready to move sites tomorrow, but it has rained quite heavily since we arrived back.

| Day 85 | Tuesday 27th May 2014 | Moy Bridge to Pattack Falls | 13 miles |

Leaving Bob's car at Moy Bridge we walked back to rejoin the East Highland Way, which headed across and round to run alongside Loch Laggan. Across moorland to begin with and then on a forest track with good views of the Loch. The day was bright, with a few clouds at first, and the sun on the mountain tops with the snow catching the light was a splendid sight. Difficult to capture the majesty of it all on camera, but we tried.

The route stayed above the loch for several miles, with silver birch trees on the shore line and fir tree plantations above. The rocky cliff, formed when the track was widened, showed the varying rock strata which was very impressive at times.

After a while we had more conifer trees, many of these were very old and extremely tall, dwarfing us mere mortals. We had a coffee stop along this track, sitting on an old fallen tree. Carrying on, we eventually came to change direction, leaving the loch for a while and going uphill through forestry plantations belonging to Ardverikie House (TV series Monarch of the Glen) On reaching

the top of the hillside we came out to grassy moorland and another loch, shown in our guide book as Lochan an H-Earba. Although this was a slight deviation from the route it was so worth while as it was stunningly beautiful and peaceful here and made the most perfect, and idyllic, lunch stop.

Dragging ourselves reluctantly away from here we headed downhill, following the stream, before turning and walking uphill for a while eventually passing the Ardverikie Saw Mills. After this the route gradually descended to Loch Laggan and we had sight of its sandy beach at the eastern end.

From here it was level walking on a good track until we reach Pattack Bridge. It was lovely to be out in open countryside again after the dark pine plantations, and we enjoyed the mountain scenery once more. At Pattack Bridge sustenance was required in the form of flapjacks: the last of them this holiday, and once fortified we continued along the A86 for a short while through a rocky outcrop, at the end of which was Pattack Falls, which are quite spectacular.

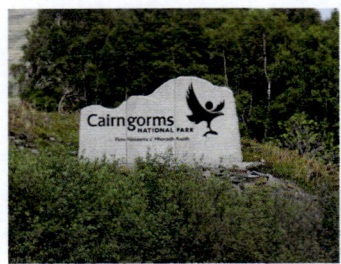

The cool water at the bottom of the falls was tempting me, and it was great to take off my boots and socks and have a refreshing paddle. The sun came out again here and it was a good end to today's section of the walk. However, on our journey back to site heavy rain accompanied us, so we were lucky to have stayed dry on the walk – we made it back just in time.

Day 86 **Wednesday 28th May 2014** **Pattack Falls to Newtonmore** **14.1 miles**

Although the forecast predicted sunshine for Newtonmore, it didn't quite happen. There was misty, showery rain to begin with this morning. However, apart from the odd brief shower it was dry for the rest of the day, although the sun never quite made it through the clouds. We left Pattack Bridge along a track parallel to the A86 but gradually leaving the road and heading uphill on a track through woodland, with views of Strathmashie House.

We entered woodland and headed uphill, near to an old Pictish fort above us. The track broadened as we approached parked forestry lorries, and then we turned onto a tarmac lane which took us across green and lush pasture land, with the mountain fells beyond, to the village of Laggan.

When we drove past Laggan, earlier in the day, there was mention of a coffee shop – however, true to 'LeJog' fashion it was no longer open. We sat on a nearby seat, and had our own flasks of coffee instead, before continuing along the A86 for a short while to take a lane on the left up to Balgowan where, passing the occasional small cottage and smallholding, we headed uphill to a forest track by a stream. We headed uphill through the woodland for quite a while and eventually came out on the high moorland: Strath an Eilich.

Crossing a very rickety bridge (twice: as we missed the path to begin with) we headed out on to the moorland and headed further uphill to evidence of an old croft near two windswept trees.

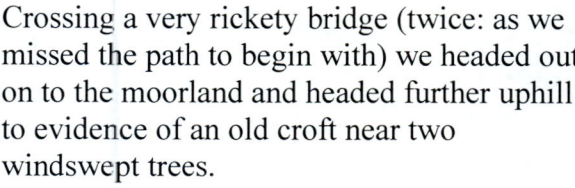

173

Here we headed across the moorland on a small track going uphill all the while until we reached the wider stony track through Cluny Estate: a wide expanse of bleak windswept moorland. We found a sheltered spot by some rocks to have our picnic lunch, and then continued downhill on the long and winding track for a few miles until we reached the stalker's bothy of Dalnashallog.

There was a challenge here as we had to cross the wide river, boulder hopping, and it took a while of looking up and downstream before finding a place to cross without us getting too wet! We eventually made it across and continued on across marshy and boggy ground to reach Dalballoch: a ruined croft. Here there was another river to cross: by the same method as before.

Again we all made it, but feet were a little damp. From here we followed a small rough track, in places picking our way across the boggy ground and smaller streams until we reached a firmer path along the River Calder. We saw many curlews here and skylarks too. Dexter had a great time chasing across the moorland after them. He must have run several miles further than us today. The sun came out briefly and it was a pretty scene alongside the river.

After a while the path improved, taking us through a forest where we stopped for a short while. There were red deer here. Through a gate at the far side of the wood we came out on a track to a bridge across the river (so 'no wet feet' this time). Now we had firmer going on a tarmac road through very pretty scenery down to Newtonmore. We were on the lower fells above the River Calder, which was deep down in the valley from here. Silver birch trees on the slopes down to the river. At a viewpoint we saw more deer grazing by the river below us.

On down to Newtonmore into the Wild Cat area: models of wild cats in and around the houses and gardens as we entered the village. Back to the car and a drive to Kingussie for a meal of fish and chips before retrieving Bob's car from Pattack Bridge, and coming back to site.

Day 87 **Monday 26ᵗʰ May 2014** **Newtonmore to Ruthven Barracks** **7 miles**

We left Newtonmore and walked through the village in an easterly direction, along the road at first, then footpath, until we reached the Folk Museum. Here we took a path named the Wildcat Trail, which went uphill through a very pretty valley: a stream below, and then a waterfall with gorse flowering profusely on the hillside.

It was a picturesque scene, albeit in showery rain at first. The track continued over sheep grazed moorland, all the while going uphill until we reached woodland where the track turned eastwards. As we climbed there were magnificent views of the mountains surrounding the Insh Valley and across to the Grampians to the east. There were rain clouds around giving some amazing cloud formations above the mountains.

We followed the edge of the woodland, at the end of which we headed downhill for a short while before turning across moorland in a more north-easterly direction, briefly, towards Loch Gynack. This was a very pretty path as we descended to the loch, with heather, bilberries, and silver birch trees here and there.

Through a more densely wooded area of silver birch next, on a small path, gradually heading uphill to a viewpoint. A brief 'flapjack stop' now, as we'd been walking for two hours, and then we were heading towards Kingussie Golf Course through more woodland, on a boarded walkway for a while, and then on a rocky path down to a caravan park.

From here we came out on to a road, briefly, before turning alongside the burn on the Gynack Mill Trail path into Kingussie. In Kingussie we took the road and then footpath towards the ruined Ruthven Barracks, passing a lovely glade of pink flowers among some young trees. A shorter walk today as we had moved site this morning.

Day 88   **Thursday 29th May 2014**   **Ruthven Barracks to Kincraig**   **8.5 miles**

We went up to the ruins of Ruthven Barracks before setting off on our route to Kincraig. The barracks sit on a mound above the Insh marshes with the town of Kingussie in the distance: the red and white of the high school dominating the view of town.

After seeing the ruins we set off uphill along the road towards the RSPB Insh Marshes Reserve, and the start of the Badenoch way, which we followed all day to Kincraig. Now on the opposite side of the marshes to Kingussie this was very attractive countryside. We were on higher ground above the marshlands and the path meandered through silver birch woodland: many of the silver birch branches were covered with pretty lichens. There were many wild flowers around and I decided to photograph some of these today.

After a while of walking through this woodland we came out at a viewpoint. We had to retrace our steps here to go downhill, heading out onto more open ground alongside the River Tromie. We followed the river for a while, through more woodland, before coming out at a road up to the old stone-built Tromie Bridge.

Looking down from the bridge gave a wonderful view of the waterfall below.

We were then were on a forest track which became more open as we reached the hamlet of Drumguish, and we were amongst cottages: quite spread out along the track. Then back into more woodland, conifers mainly but later this changed to silver birches, juniper bushes, heather and bilberries. We arrived at a viewpoint to the Cairngorm mountain range, where we stopped on a thoughtfully provided wooded bench to have our coffee.

Descending along the track from here we came out to open ground and the hamlet of Inveruglass. There were a some new, modern and stylish houses here. We walked along a track behind the gardens of some of these dwellings, admiring the various architecture as we went. The track here had many juniper bushes alongside, together with flowering broom, so it was a pretty path.

At the end of this track we passed another grand house before turning right, uphill on a forestry track. This then turned left, and we continued until we reached a smaller path off to the left, which took us through more dense woodland, with more wild flowers, eventually leading to duck boards over the boggy ground onto a firmer wider track. Along a small track next to the road before then crossing the road into the RSPB Reserve, the forest paths taking us down to the water's edge of Loch Insh. There was another bench seat here and this was a good place to have our lunch overlooking the loch. After lunch, still following the Badenoch Way, the track took us uphill on a small path up stone steps, eventually coming out again on the road.

A few yards along here and we turned left down a stony track, behind a very grandly designed large timber and glass house, down to the Water Sports Centre on Loch Insh. We continued past the Centre and carried on to the end of the loch. The bridge over the river Spey at the end of the loch was impressive with its wooden piers supporting the long bridge.

We then took the road for a short distance into Kincraig, turning off to look at Insh Church, and spotting an osprey flying overhead as we were nearing the church.

Crossing the bridge we reached Kincraig and the village shop, where we enjoyed an ice cream before heading to the car.

Back to Ruthven to collect Bob's car, we then all went to visit the Highland Folk Museum at Newtonmore before coming back to site. A more gentle day today, and good dry weather, although cloudy this morning. The sun came out late afternoon and this evening looks quite settled, so we hope for a good day tomorrow for our last section of the East Highland Way to Aviemore.

Day 89   **Friday 30th May 2014**   **Kincraig to Aviemore**   **10.5 miles**

We awoke to blue skies and sunshine this morning: the promise of a really fine day. Leaving Kincraig we passed through by a small farm before heading through gates up on a track to high woodland, eventually above the River Freshie, and then on a track uphill to woodland and the Frank Bruce Sculpture Trail. We had a look at some of the sculptures: all made from either wood or stone, but mainly in wood. They were nearly all figures or faces carved from the wood, each with a description by the sculptor. He appears to have been a man with a troubled mind judging by some of the ideas behind his work.

We carried on through forest, still above the river, until we reached a downhill track to Freshie Bridge. This was a stone bridge: dated from 18th century, above a very deep river and today there were swimmers in the cold water (in wet suits). Once across the bridge we continued up the road until we reached the top of the hill at Heather Brae. Here we entered a large area of forest, and it took quite a bit of navigating by Bob and Andy as we walked through this section.

There were views through the woodland across to the still snow-capped Cairngorm mountain, and then later we came out of the forest plantations into more native woodland, with small conifers bordering the sandy, rocky path. Passing a woodland glade we came across Drake's bothy, and we sat here to have our coffee, and enjoy the sunshine, before heading off once again.

We passed Loch Gamhna on our left and when we reached the end we crossed the river outflow from the loch. It was stunningly beautiful here, the reflections alone were worth a couple of photos: it makes such a difference when the sun is out!

On from Loch Gamhna we continued uphill to go through more native woodland, on yet another pretty path, and we soon reached Loch an Eilein. This was a well visited local attraction, with a path around the loch and a visitor centre. We sat at the end of the loch to have our lunch and it was a delightful spot to stay for a while. Reluctantly leaving the loch we headed on a wider track past some cottages before reaching another small loch, Lochan Mor, a man made 'lily' loch, with views to the mountains behind.

We reached a bridge over the Spey before arriving at a road and cycle track into Aviemore.

Once in Aviemore we sought out the end of the East Highland Way: where the Speyside Way begins at its southernmost point, and then took a photo of the four of us.

Day 90   **Saturday 31st May 2014**   **Aviemore to near Carrbridge**   **13.75 miles**

We woke to another dry day: some cloud, but with the promise of warm temperatures. We left Aviemore to head up the Burma Road (track) over the fells and down onto a lane heading for Carrbridge, where we'd left our car for the return journey.

The track was wide and stony for the most part, and at first went between woodland and the native silver birch trees and heather. It was a continuous uphill climb for several miles coming out from the woodland and onto the open moor, with heather and bilberries growing here.

Passing several shooting posts for the grouse season as we climbed, and with stunning views back to the still snow topped mountains of the Cairngorms, we eventually made it to a memorial stone near the summit of our climb. After stopping to check the route, and taking a photo of the four of us, we then had a downhill path for several miles: we could see it stretching out before us. Crossing a small tributary, we then headed down to the valley of the River Dalmain. The bridge over the river was wide, as was the stony river bed. We stopped here to have our lunch: another very beautiful spot, very peaceful with the occasional cry from grouse, or curlew overhead.

From here we took the track towards Carrbridge through heathery moorland to begin with and then across grassland with juniper trees.

Lynne and I were looking at the various birds: oyster catcher, curlew and lapwing, and, we think, a stonechat: but we'll have to look this one up to make sure. Still recording the many wild flowers that are out as we go too.

After a few miles we reached the river crossing: no bridge and too deep to boulder hop, it was down to bare feet and paddling now.

Quite difficult, as the rocks in the river bed were very slippery, and even with a walking pole it was difficult to make anything other than slow progress.

The men reached the other side first and didn't contain their amusement at Lynne and me struggling to make it over too. Bob took many photos to record the event, hoping no doubt that one of us would get wetter than we wanted!

Dexter of course had no trouble getting across and enjoyed a good swim while he waited for us. Prior to that he had flushed out a red deer and a few grouse to keep him happy.

From the river crossing we took a lane for about a mile and a half to get back to our car, our clothes drying on us as we walked: fortunately it was sunny. We reached the car, which was parked by the cycle-way sign to Slaggan Bridge: and this is where we shall start walking from tomorrow.

Drove into Carrbridge to look at the famous old bridge and to have a cup of tea and cake in the coffee shop. Back from there to site, we took down awnings ready to move tomorrow afternoon after the walk. This evening we had a lovely meal in Kingussie at 'The Tipsy Laird' which was a good end to the day.

Day 91   Sunday 1st June 2014   Near Carrbridge to Findhorn Bridge, Tomatin   7 miles

A short walk through woodland at first brought us out to Slaggan Bridge, where we crossed the river and took a pretty path through open woodland.

Slaggan Bridge

Path after Slaggan Bridge

A view back

There were good views back over the countryside we'd walked through yesterday. We were heading for the railway viaduct, where we stopped to have our coffee, before continuing on toward the road and the summit of the railway at Slochd. A lane towards Tomatin took us downhill and we finished our walk today: and for this year, at Findhorn Bridge in the Findhorn Valley. There was nowhere safe to balance the camera to take a group photo, so we had to suffice with a photo of each couple: not forgetting 7 month old Dexter dog.

Lynne and Bob

Meg, Andy and Dexter at Findhorn Bridge, near Tomatin

1,219 miles walked since Land's End

Day 92   **Monday 3rd May 2015**   **Findhorn Bridge to Farr**   **14.53 miles**

Much improved weather today after yesterday's wind, rain, snow showers, and temperatures of 5 degrees! Today was bright and breezy, sunny for the most part: although we did have some light rain in the wind on occasions, but not for long. We put one car at Woodside, near Farr, and then drove in Bob's car to Findhorn Bridge near Tomatin where we had finished our walking last year. After taking the obligatory, and now traditional, start of walk photo, we took a lane west along the Findhorn valley.

This was pretty with the river below us as we climbed gently up along the side of the valley. There were good views to be had as we walked the five miles to our right turn at Garbole. We stopped at the bridge over Allt Beag for a short break, before turning north-west uphill on a lane.

It was here that we had our first sighting of a golden eagle. Soaring in the sky above our heads, we could see the markings on the wings, and the huge wingspan.

Along the lane uphill and then through woodland for a while until we reached open moorland: a bleak and barren landscape, heather mainly, but not yet in flower, and we made our way up and over the moor to Farr Wind Farm at Carn Odhar.

There were 39 huge wind turbines up here on this vast area of moorland. Views back showed the snow covered Cairngorm Mountains as we climbed. At the Wind Farm we found a shooting hut near the summit of Carn Odhar, and we made use of the shelter to eat our picnic lunch out of the wind, which was quite fresh and strong at this altitude.

We were at 1843 feet above sea level here. We made our way on a gravel track passing several wind turbines at close range as we headed to lower ground to a lane along the bottom of a valley. It was much warmer here out of the wind, and with a blue sky above us it was very pleasant. There was some cloud throughout the day but it was so much better than when we arrived yesterday.

Carrying on along the lane there were some beautiful beech trees that were just about to break into leaf and it was easy walking here along the lane.

Further along there were rhododendrons, which I know are a nuisance because they stop anything else growing, but they are also pretty when they flower. We walked on until we came to Loch Farr: amidst woodland alongside the lane, and a little further on from here was our waiting car.

Day 93   **Tuesday 5th May 2015**   **Farr to Inverness**   **10.5 miles**

From Woodside, near Farr, we walked up a lane and then downhill to pass a very grand 'castle-like' house with turrets before crossing the River Nairn just below on a very old stone bridge.

Then on a good track up to woodland where we saw two deer. Walking through the forest was pleasant and we came across Loch Buchanton where Dexter had a great time retrieving sticks. We had a coffee stop there (from our flasks – no coffee shops here) before going out onto farmland and heading uphill to join a lane, which we followed for several miles through gorse and heather clad hillside.

Weather getting increasingly wetter. Nowhere to have lunch: we ended up sitting in a bus shelter on the outskirts of Inverness to have our sandwiches! Arrived at the car, by the river in Inverness, and then back to site, via Tesco's for food shopping. Raining more steadily all afternoon and evening, but another 10.5 miles done.

Day 94   Wednesday 6th May 2015   Inverness to Knockbain (Reelig Glen)   14 miles

We left our car in a woodland car park at Knockbain. Then, in Bob's car, drove back to Inverness to start the walk. As we were leaving the woodland car park, along the lane, Andy spotted a red squirrel who obligingly stayed a while, so we all saw it. On arriving in Inverness, we started off along by the River Ness and, after looking at the magnificent and thought provoking war memorial, we crossed the bridge to walk along the river to the Cathedral: St Andrews. Although small, as cathedrals go, it was a lovely warm red stone building with golden timber inside. There were some Russian Icons on display: given to the cathedral by Alexander the Great of Russia. Also two watercolours of the architect's design for the cathedral, which was originally depicted with two steeples: one on each of the towers. For whatever reason the steeples were never built. There was also beautiful stained glass: in particular the West Front window.

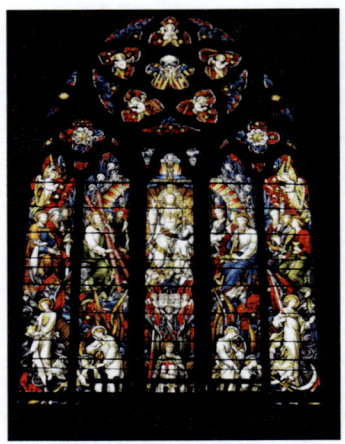

After admiring the Cathedral we walked along the river to cross at the next bridge to reach the Castle, which is now the Sheriff's Courts. There has been a castle on this site since the 800s, although many different castles have been built on the site depending upon how often it was attacked over the years! A statue of Flora MacDonald was in the courtyard in front of the Castle. And just along from here was the start of the Great Glen Way. Moving on from the castle we took the Great Glen Way alongside the River Ness and crossed the river on a series of bridges between islands, on good pathways landscaped with mature trees and rhododendrons – very green.

There were sculptured wooden seats – all different – and even a fallen tree made into 'Nessy' the Loch Ness Monster. We came to the bridge over the Caledonian Canal and followed the canal for a short while, before leaving it to walk uphill for several miles, passing what could have been an old workhouse – a vast stone built impressive building. It was all boarded up and there was no way of knowing its history.

Still heading uphill we reached woodland, on a very pretty path through silver birches, firs and beech trees, all covered with lichen which gave them quite a ghostly appearance. (Lichen only grows on trees where the air is very clear). We went through this woodland for quite some miles, and still uphill.

Then after our lunch break, sat on some logs at the side of the path, *(still raining)*, we continued, missing our way for a while and having to retrace our steps, until we came out of the woodland heading downhill. So many fallen trees today, some of which blocked our way and it became a bit of an obstacle course. There has been some bad weather up here recently to cause all this damage.

Once at the bottom of the wood we were on a track passing grand houses – of varying architectural styles – and then we turned left along a lane, and there were magnificent views. The rain stopped, and we could see the impressive view of Beauly Firth and the snow-covered mountains beyond: many mountain ranges.

The weather today was drizzly and not that warm, and we had waterproofs on all day. Towards the end of the walk we did have about an hour without rain, and the sun did try to come out. It remained cold – only 8 or 9 degrees today. At least the clouds lifted at the end of the walk so that we could see the views. It would have been a really lovely day's walk if the weather had been sunny and warm.

Day 95   Friday 8th May 2015   Knockbain (Reelig Glen) to Ruisauire   10.6 miles

Leaving Bob's car at Reelig Glen, we walked up through the woods, having to negotiate more fallen trees: and there were many tree casualties here. Beautiful beech tree woodlands after that until we reached the road, passing a log cabin – Reelig Glen Community Forest.

Along a lane and out to magnificent views of the higher ground and snow-capped mountains. Walking between green pastureland with the mountains beyond was magical – and we had some lovely sunny weather today to enjoy it all. It was good to see blue skies, and this lifted our

spirits considerably after the cold wet days we've had. A short stop to admire a view and have our coffee, before descending to Tomnacross, where there was a large chapel and a thriving looking school.

Down the path to the village of Kiltarlity, turning right on the road before entering some forest to our left and heading to cross the river. However, the bridge had gone, and we made the decision to walk further around into the Beaufort Castle Estate, where we joined a driveway and then a footpath to Home Farm. Here there was a bridge and a stone wall which we sat upon to have our lunch, after which we headed uphill and along the road to a large bridge over the River Beauly.

We passed some magnificent beech woods today, with their new bright green leaves. The sunlight coming through the tree canopy was beautiful.

We made our way along the road for a while to Kilmorack Gallery, before turning uphill toward Broallan, where there were more views as we climbed. A short drink stop at the top of the hill, and then lane walking to Ruisauire where there were excellent panoramic views of Beauly Firth down to Inverness and to the Moray Firth.

Day 96   **Saturday 9th May 2015**   **Ruisaurie to Marybank**   **9.2 miles**

Leaving Bob's car at Ruisaurie we walked along the lane for a short distance before crossing a stream and turning left uphill on a track through native trees, mainly silver birch, then coming out into the open onto moorland where there were fantastic mountain views to be had. We crossed the moorland to reach Loch nam Bonnach, taking a track round the north of the Loch.

This track became very difficult and then non-existent as we made our way through heather and rough grasses avoiding the boggy bits as best we could. It was tough going as the grassy mounds became further apart and the ground wetter. We reached a fence which we climbed, thinking that this was to take us toward a second track. However we had to retrace our steps back to the fence, and take a slightly different route across the rough ground. Eventually, and walking on a compass bearing, we made our way towards where we hoped we would see another loch. To make it

even more challenging one of the step stiles had no steps, just wires across which we had to climb up and through – no easy feat. Then, shortly after that, in the distance we could see a grassy bank and we headed for that spot to have a coffee break. On arriving at the bank we were also at the Loch nan Eun. We enjoyed sitting on the grassy bank and having our coffee and the views there were fantastic: mountain peaks reflected in the loch, and a feeling of being on top of the world.

From there we had to get to a track on the other side of the overflow outlet from the loch. We had to cross a ledge, water flowing over this, to get to the other side. Much laughter as we each made it over, and with Bob taking photos as we did so! It was a short distance now over more rough moorland before we made it to a firm track.

This track took us downhill to Auchmore Wood, a fir tree plantation. We found a way into the wood on a track near electric pylons, and we cut down the hillside to reach a track which was on our map and which took us out of the forest to Aultgowrie Bridge. We crossed the river at the bridge and then sat to have our lunch, sitting on a stone wall at the edge of the lane. Carrying on down the lane we reached the River Orrin, which we crossed on a large stone bridge.

The clouds were gathering and looking rather menacing, and as we walked down the lane to Marybank, there was a cloudburst of hailstones: the temperature plummeted for a short while until the hail stopped, and we were all rather wet when we reached the waiting car at Marybank.

The weather today had otherwise been glorious, with blue skies to start, with and the temperature was comfortable for walking. As the day progressed, the cloud was building over the mountains resulting in the hailstorm.

Back at site, which is next to the football ground for Ross County, there was a match and much cheering and loud noise coming from the stands.

This evening we had a meal at The National Hotel in Dingwall, which was very good. As we returned to site Bob slipped off the kerb, while avoiding the crowds leaving the football ground, and managed to injure his leg – we're not sure if it's a pulled muscle, or worse.

| Day 97 | Thursday 7th May 2015 | Marybank to Dingwall | 6.6 miles |

Drove to Marybank and parked our car.

We left Marybank along a lane, crossing over the River Conon on the long and narrow Moy Bridge. There were notices warning of sudden rising water when the river was prone to flooding and there was a wide flood plain down this valley.

Our walk took us along the main road for a while but soon we were pleased to turn right, away from this, and follow a track between meadows, with young lambs around in some. We paused to look at a monument giving us the legend of a folklore tale about two sisters who were killed in the 18th Century: and how this had been predicted way back in the 17th Century!

Along the track for a while until we came to the Brahan Estate, passing a grand house and, opposite, an old gateway.

Some lovely snowdrops there: if that is what they were, as they were very tall, more the height of daffodils, but certainly snowdrop-type flowers.

Along a track from here to another farm building – quite imposing with a large clock tower. Further on from this we passed the Caravan Club Site *(CL)* before turning left up a long track between woodland, and many piles of timber.

Good views to be had on our left (north west) to the mountains – still snow covered at the top. At a site of some deforestation we sat in the sunshine on some logs to have a snack, until the hailstones came again. It has been very cold today, prolonged periods of sunshine between some short sharp hail showers. Temperature about 8 degrees again, at best.

We reached the village of Maryburgh and then walked along the cycle track to Dingwall, passing a huge cattle market, outside of which was a large sculpture of a farmer with his Highland cow and dog. On our arrival at site we decided on a fish and chip supper tonight, as it was quite late by now.

Day 98 Monday 11th May 2015 Dingwall to Evanton 10.6 miles

We had a day off yesterday, mainly due to poor weather, and decided to go to church in the town – we went to the Scottish Presbyterian Free Church service in Dingwall, which was lovely. Other than that we gave Dexter short walks when the rain eased, and got some washing done.

We left Dingwall just after 9 am, walking from site. We went through the town and then uphill *very steeply* on a lane following the Dochcarty Burn: walking uphill from 20 metres to 202 metres above sea level in 2.5 miles. Good views to be had back to the south and west as we climbed.

We followed this lane steadily uphill, now onto more open ground and passing small cottages and crofts as we headed up to the moor through pastureland: young calves and cattle, and many sheep with their lambs. The weather had been fine and sunny to begin with but clouds began to build from the west and soon we had to put on waterproofs.

This was how the day went: waterproofs off and then on. However, at least there were some brighter spells so that we could see the scenery. Leaving the cows and sheep behind we were out on rougher moorland, with a more difficult path which came out to a river below us: an impressive ox-bow here that had nearly become a full circle. On through the forest, meeting up with our next track, which pleased Bob who was navigating.

There were many fallen trees in the forest which needed negotiating again today. Once on the forestry track we started heading downhill, eventually coming out of the forest and into pastureland with small farms.

When the sun came out we could see many oil rigs in the distance in Cromarty Firth. Our track took us into the small town of Evanton where we finished our walk, going through the village to reach our waiting car. We saw a red kite soaring overhead.

Bob was struggling a bit at the end: the result of a pulled muscle on Saturday evening, which was rather painful. We weren't sure until this morning if he'd be fit to walk at all today.

Day 99   Wednesday 13th May 2015   Evanton to Ardross Church   13.8 miles

Well, what an eventful walk this turned out to be! We started off well enough along a lane from Evanton, going west before taking a track through woodland for quite a few miles. Difficult to navigate, but we managed, and we were rewarded with our steady and long climb by magnificent views of the mountains inland and of Cromarty Firth below us, with the oil rigs being a prominent feature in the landscape here. We could see right back to the distant Cairngorm Mountains and, ahead of us, views along the Cromarty Firth.

We were walking behind and round a large hill (453 metres above sea level), at the top of which was a strange monument. We took the path up to the top, although it meant going off the route briefly. It was worth the climb – such amazing views here. The stone structure of arches and columns made for an impressive landscape. We took a group photo here, before returning the way we'd climbed back to our route.

We were back through woodland on a good path, or it would have been if so many fallen trees had not blocked it: we had to climb under, over, or around many of these. Dexter went off on a chase of something or other too while we were otherwise occupied in making our way. We stopped for lunch, and Dexter finally returned, puffing and panting – he must have gone a distance.

After lunch, more forestry tracks, until we eventually started to descend through timber stacks along a track for a mile or so down to the River Alness.

A beautiful spot at Hoch Pool

At Hoch Pool, we had a flapjack stop – *just as well, given what was to follow!*

(Top right photo) A little further upstream was a footbridge that we needed to cross over the river – but the last section of bridge was missing: from an island to the bank. The river was flowing fast here too. There was a fallen tree partly across the river here and Andy managed, just, to get to the bank opposite – the tree trunk wasn't that safe.

In the fast flowing water below, Andy spotted a ladder-type metal structure, which was part of the bridge. Andy managed to hook a long branch into the ladder and bring it to the surface, pulling it through the fast flowing water, and gradually get it onto the bank. With Bob hanging from another tree on the opposite bank, and grabbing the ladder as it came near, they eventually got the ladder to straddle between the tree trunk and bank.

(Photo 2nd on right)
Bob then found the old hand rail of the previous bridge on his side of the river. Between them Andy and Bob managed to hold this rail above the ladder, so that Lynne and I could get across, *(Photo 3rd on right)* both of them holding the hand rail and ladder firm. *Meantime Dexter tried to swim across the river, and just made it by clinging on to the ladder rails, that were still in the water at that time, and fighting against the fast flowing water.*

(Photo 4th on right) Then Bob had to get across – there was no-one left on the bank to hold the handrail for Bob and so Andy held the ladder firm, and Bob crawled across on his hands and knees. All safely across.

But then we had further problems, as the footpath we were now on was made difficult by the many fallen trees across our route, and another missing and broken bridge, seen in this photograph.

Added to which the slope down to the fast flowing river on our left below us was very steep, and made for hazardous conditions as we tried to get across or around the fallen trees without further mishap.

It made for slow and arduous going, and a very slow section for us. Eventually, as there were several fallen trees ahead of us making the going even more treacherous, we decided it would be easier (relatively speaking) to head up the steep slope to our right, as it seemed there was flatter and more open ground at the top of the slope. It was tough going – on hands and knees, and sliding on bottoms occasionally, as we painstakingly made our way up to this more level ground.

Then a short distance between two fences, to a place where we hoped to get across into a field and up to a lane. With barbed wire on the fences it was a difficult thing to do. Bob used Lynne's jacket to cover the barbed wire so that I could climb over. Hoping for an easier route, Lynne went under the fence causing much hilarity as, once under, Lynne couldn't move as she was laughing so much. (I think the strain of the last few miles had something to do with it!)

With relief, we reach the lane and the short distance back to the car

Eventually we were all through and headed across a field up to the lane, where on safe ground we walked the mile or so back to our car, which was parked opposite Ardross Church.

We had a meal at The National Hotel in Dingwall tonight. **We deserved it!!!**

Day 100   **Thursday 21st May 2015**   **Ardross Church to Wester Fearn**   **14 miles**

We parked near Ardross Church (not in the large, and empty, church car park, as it was not allowed!) and started our walk along the lane, through forest, and above the River Alness, which had caused us problems with a broken bridge on the last section.

At the end of Inchlumpie Forest we were in Strath Rusdale, and we eventually came to a cottage and a pretty stream on our right. We stopped here for our coffee before heading uphill to a forestry enclosure, where we went through a very narrow gate, and then followed the fence, making our way across the first stream of the day.

We followed the fence-line as far as we could, and then turned right to follow the edge of the plantation, until we reached another gate on to high moorland. Here we saw two red deer.
Then began the 7 miles of moorland, with no tracks, Bob and Andy did a great job in navigating on

compass bearings and GPS to get us across this large section of the walk. It was very hard going, and it was difficult to avoid some of the wet and boggy areas. We had several streams and peat ditches to cross today, many of which were 'check-points' for Bob, to get our bearings.

After lunch we were relieved to find some sort of 'vague' track, which came and went on the ground depending upon the ground conditions! Way in the distance, we were aiming for a hut with a red roof, and then after that a river, which we came to after making our way down a steep heathery bank.

Once at this river there was a proper track, which was lovely, and a relief to Lynne and me at least.

Down this track past a bridge and dam at a cottage, 'Upper Garvery', and down towards trees. We passed a magnificent waterfall on our left, 'Eas a Chobhaim Duibh', and then we descended to Dornoch Firth, which was very pretty, going through gorse, and silver birch, and with great views to admire on our way. Eventually we reached the road and our waiting car at an AA box.

We were all very weary as it had been a hard day's walk of 14 miles.

Day 101   **Tuesday 19th May 2015**   **Wester Fearn to Loch Buidhe**   **11 miles**

Parking Bob's car at Wester Fearn by an AA Box – a rare sight nowadays – along the Dornoch Firth, we started off in cold but dry weather, although there were many clouds around us. There was no option other than to road walk for a while, until we found our track through a farm and then running parallel to the road. Passing through a field of Highland Cattle, we were then on a track which led to a stream and a ford (fortunately this was not a difficult crossing).

The track then rejoined the road and we had a view of Dornoch Firth, and Bonar Bridge crossing the narrowest point of the Firth. Before that we reached Kincardine Church, unfortunately locked, as there was a Pictish stone that would have been interesting to see. However, there was a picture and description of it on the church wall outside. We continued on along the road through Ardgay, and then were on the long approach to Bonar Bridge.

Arriving at the bridge, we stopped at the loch-side for our coffee, before heading out of Bonar Bridge uphill. Bonar Bridge is a modern construction, but there were descriptions of two previous bridges on plaques on the far side of the bridge.

Going uphill in a northerly direction we were on a lane, with increasing views as we walked. We reached a view to Loch Migdale,

and then we were among construction traffic for 5 miles, many heavy lorries carrying aggregate, and much heavy plant doing various jobs along this section. All the drivers of the trucks and lorries seemed a jolly bunch, giving us a wave as we passed. At one point, there was a bridge missing, and we were initially told we couldn't get through. Talking to one of the construction workers, who seemed to have authority, he asked where we were headed, and told us that the diversion would mean a further four miles walk for us. We must have looked fairly dismayed at this because he then said that he'd have a look and see if he could get us across. This he did, and we were very grateful. With a cheery wave he sent us on our way, and we headed uphill, finding a spot to have our picnic lunch before we were out in the open moorland, and before the impending rain arrived.

We spent the next three miles or so, giving way to diggers and lorries as they made their busy way across the moor,

.... and then the rain came ... very cold, with sleet. There was a relentless downpour all the way to the car at the end of Loch Buidhe.

Day 102 Wednesday May 20th 2015 Loch Buidhe to Golspie 12 miles

We parked Bob's car at Loch Buidhe in very different weather conditions to yesterday. The sun was out and although there was a fresh breeze, it was lovely to have blue skies and to see the scenery. We left the Loch to walk down a narrow lane, along which we encountered little traffic today. To begin with crossing moorland and following the river as it meandered its way down the valley. The views were good today.

After a mile or so we passed an isolated white cottage, the only sign of habitation in that bleak landscape, then still carrying on down the valley, we finally came to silver birch and rowan trees, all thickly coated in green lichen. The river was close to us at times, meandering as it found its way. It was lovely to see blue sky reflected in the water.

Then lower down, there were more trees and the ground levelled out, the river rippling along beside us, and a couple of ford crossings to a farm were seen. We had our coffee sat at the side of the lane, in the warm sunshine. As we came down the valley we lost the chilly wind and it was a very pleasant change to yesterday's cold rain and sleet.

Still following the river we came to a waterfall on the opposite hillside, which was quite dramatic as it fell over huge rocky outcrops to the river below.

The lane was more gentle in descent now and quite straight as we approached the Causeway and the A9 over Loch Fleet. At the side of the lane it was very wet ground, with irises and marsh marigolds, or king cups, and reeds growing in the standing water.

There was no option at the causeway but to walk alongside the road, the busy A9, and we were hoping to find a way through to Loch Fleet Nature Reserve away from the A9: otherwise it would have meant some horrible road walking.

We were fortunate to find a path through to the railway, which we crossed to reach the Loch-side and the wood. To begin with this path was between much flowering gorse and the scent was very strong, and pleasant, as we walked through. There were climbers nearby making use of some good rock-climbing crags. Once over the railway, we were able to gain access to a track into the Nature Reserve.

We followed tracks through here until we reached a lane, which we followed into Golspie, passing the golf course on the coast on the way. It was a long straight section of road for over a mile until we reached the town: it seemed a long way before we finally reached our car.

Day 103   **Thursday 14th May 2015**   **Golspie to Brora**   **7.5 miles**

Having arrived at site at Brora, we had lunch and then drove to Golspie to walk back along the coastal path back to site. We started off crossing the river in Golspie on a pretty wooden bridge and by an impressive mill with a circular tower.

Crossing a field to the coast path the very strong north-easterly breeze made it feel quite chilly, but the sun was shining, the sea was very blue and the crests of the waves were very white. It is the first time we've walked along a beach since Sennen Cove near Land's End.

Further along the coast we saw the much pinnacled castle of Dunrobin, set upon the hillside next to the sea. Up on the fells behind  the castle was a large statue of the Duke of Sutherland (responsible for the Highland Clearances in the 19th century, and now the general feeling is that the statue of this man should be removed).

The route then took us through the castle grounds through woodland, with primroses and bluebells, and still lovely views of the sea to our right. In the distance was land this side of the Moray Firth.

We came out of the woodland and continuing along the coast through fields and then along to Doll Beach we arrived at a waterfall on our left. A little further on from there, we sat out of the wind to have our drink, and flapjacks provided by Lynne (mine have all gone now).

While we were sat there, Bob noticed seals on the rocks out to sea, and then, the more you looked, the more you noticed. I zoomed in with my camera for some close up shots.

From there on it was a very exposed coastline, flat pasture with cows grazing and then pebbly beach, until we came to Brora.

Very picturesque and quaint cottages at the harbour side. Up into the town we walked and crossed the impressive, high, stone bridge over the River Brora.

Then out towards the sea again, with good views of the harbour at a viewpoint, where there was a toposcope.

Along the side of the golf course for about a mile and a half, with impressive sea views as we walked, and then across the golf course to the site and our caravans, after a bracing walk that certainly blew any cobwebs away!

Bob's leg is very painful; he has contacted NHS 24, and Lynne has now driven him to Golspie Hospital. We shan't be walking tomorrow

Day 104   **Monday 18th May 2015**   **Brora to Lothbeg**   **4.6 miles**

We've had quite a gap in our walking, as Bob is injured with a poorly leg, which required him to be seen at Golspie Hospital on our arrival at Brora: there is an infection, and he has to have antibiotics. It is questionable whether we can still achieve getting to John O' Groats this year.

After 3 days of resting, Bob says it is improving, and so we have decided to walk the 4.6 mile section today from Brora to Lothbeg, a short section to see if Bob will be able to walk OK, and without pain now.

Our route took us along the coast, on the sandy beaches of Brora Bay and along to Lothbeg, where we reach the A9, before turning north on towards Kinbrace.

The walk today was a delight. We saw so many sea birds: oyster catchers, arctic terns, eider ducks, and many gulls. We stopped

briefly as we neared Lothbeg, and a seal popped its head out of the water, and then seemed to follow us as we made our way along his beach, emerging now and then to check out the strangers on his patch. Similarly the nesting sea-birds were making quite a noise, particularly the terns and oyster catchers. While we were sat having a break on the sand dunes a large convoy of eider ducks came into view, shortly followed by another convoy coming to meet them from the opposite direction. They were so comical, as they 'spoke' to each other, it was just like long lost relatives meeting each other and catching up with the latest gossip, they were really funny to listen to.

Towards the end of our walk the tide was coming in and we had to go higher up the beach, onto the pebbles, seaweed and rocks, to avoid getting our feet wet. As we approached Lothbeg we neared the railway, alongside which was a pretty grassy bank covered with primroses. It was here that we came across an adder basking in the sunshine.

Dexter had a great time today: in and out of the water chasing sticks, seagulls and anything that moved, he must have gone miles further than us. The weather was kind today too: it was warmer and dry for the whole of the walk, at least until we got back to site.

Once at the car at Lothbeg we drove to Helmsdale and sat on a bench by the harbour to enjoy a lunch of fish and chips.

Day 105 **Friday 22ⁿᵈ May 2015** **Lothbeg to Kildonan** **12.5 miles**

We started on the A9 for just a short while, from the lay-by to the turning up Glen Loth, on a narrow lane. It went steadily uphill and we could soon see the glen opening out before us, and the mountains around the glen. There was a cold and brisk northerly wind, and later on this wind brought heavy showers for a while and it was very cold and windy then. It eased off a little as we reached a stream, where we sat to have our coffee.

It rained again soon after this and although we could see views of mountain peaks all around, they were rather hazy through the cloud. The lane then followed a forestry plantation for a couple of miles, the rain easing, before heading downhill where the views of the Helmsdale Valley appeared below us.

Following Craggie Burn on a downhill track, and crossing the burn by a stone bridge, we found the perfect spot to have our lunch sat by this picturesque stream with primroses flowering around us. It was an idyllic spot, and we were reluctant to leave, especially as it was out of the wind.

The strong winds kept up for most of the walk, only easing a little in the shelter of the valley when we reached the river and railway crossing at Kildonan station. From the bridge over the Helmsdale River we had a spectacular view of this very scenic river as it tumbled over the rocks at this point.

We joined the main road through the Helsmsdale valley and the river was very pretty all along here, with many small waterfalls, as it made its way down to Helmsdale.

After a while the valley widened. We were out of the shelter of the valley now and the north wind came in with a vengeance as we made our way uphill to our waiting car.

It was a challenge staying upright at times today, but at least it stayed dry this afternoon.

We've now walked 1,370 miles since Land's End. Bob is still walking after his leg injury and says he is OK to carry on. So, reasons to celebrate, and we went to The Sutherland Inn this evening for a meal.

We leave the site at Brora tomorrow, having stayed here longer than anticipated. It is a beautiful location, and we have enjoyed being here, despite the less than perfect weather, *and our caravan awning wrecked in the high winds!*

Day 106   **Sunday 24th May 2015**   **Beyond Kildonan to Forsinard Station**   **14 miles**

It was a long drive from site at Bowermadden in Caithness-shire to our last walk point in Sutherland. The road network in this part of Scotland is very limited, due to the terrain here. We arrived at 3 miles beyond Kildonan at around 10 am to start to walk to Forsinard Station. The walk was on the road today (the A897) but, as is often the case in the far north in the mountainous areas, the A road was single track with passing places and with not too much traffic. We set off up the valley, and soon came to mountain views ahead, and vast stretches of moorland.

After the hamlet of Kinbrace we carried on up to Loch an Ruathair, a large loch, at least two miles long. We stopped for lunch just off the road, by some fir trees near a bridge and stream – so once again we had lunch by a babbling brook.

The weather today was showery: sunshine in between frequent showers that were over quite quickly, but it meant that we had to keep waterproofs on all day. There was a fresh north-westerly wind too: so hats and gloves again today. The railway was alongside us, sometimes near and sometimes the other side of the valley. Near to the road there were old timber snow fences, now not in good condition.

It was a bleak but beautiful landscape with the mountains around and we were fortunate to have some good visibility to see it today. The occasional burst of bright yellow from the gorse bushes contrasted well with the mainly brown coloured moorland.

Eventually we came to the top of the valley, and crossed the watershed into Strath Halladale, and after a couple of miles reached the Forsinard RSPB Centre in the Flow Country: the largest section of blanket bog in the world. Here, the RSPB were erecting a viewing tower over the Flow Country, a modern building which contrasted with the mountain scenery and blanket bog all around (slightly incongruous we thought). A few yards after this we reached our destination at Forsinard Station.

It was a lovely walk, and would have been even better in warmer and sunnier weather.

Day 107   **Tuesday 26th May 2015**   **Forsinard to Altnabreac**   **14 miles**

Drove to Scotscaulder Station to get the train to our starting point at Forsinard. At the station there was a thermometer which showed the temperature to be just 9 degrees C. With a strong wind, it certainly felt chilly. Dressed in the maximum amount of clothing we had with us we set off. Once at Forsinard we walked along the small 'A' road to Forsinain, where the track to Altnabreac went over the Flow Country. As we walked down the road we saw three red deer up on the moorland on our left.

We made good time to the signpost at Forsinain and started up a wide sandy track through woodland at first and then out onto the Flow Country.

The track had been cut between the peat, the height of which at the side of the track was at least 8 feet.

We were very pleased not to be walking over boggy moorland and we soon reached Loch Leih: it was pretty chilly up here, but there were good views to high peaks in the far distance.

We had 10 miles of this track, and most of it has now been deforested, the intention being to return any forest back to blanket bog. So the scenery was much the same for many miles, some areas of small pools in the peaty bog, and the only animals up here were a herd of deer in the distance. We did see the two-carriage train in the distance which seemed an incongruous sight in the wilderness here.

There were many skylarks singing above us as we walked, and we heard the occasional curlew. No cuckoo today, unlike most of the walk in Scotland when we have heard the cuckoo almost daily.

Towards the end of the walk we reached a forestry plantation at Station Hill, and it was about half a mile further on that we reached the remote station of Altnabreac. There were about five houses making up this hamlet.

The train wasn't due until 5.21pm and we had arrived at the station at 3.30pm, so we had a little wait. However there was a small wooden shelter where we could sit and get out of the wind and rain. The weather had been kinder today in that the rain showers had been fewer, but it had been a chilly day. We were pleased to board the warm train for the one stop to Scotscaulder, to our waiting car.

Day 108   Wednesday 27th May 2015   Altnabreac to Loch More   **6.5 miles**

We drove to Scotscaulder, having left one car at Loch More, and caught the 8.53 am train to Altnabreac. As yesterday, the temperature reading at Scotscaulder station was only 9 degrees C! Leaving Altnabreac, and dressed warmly, we set off along the good sandy track that we had left yesterday, in the direction of Loch More. This was mainly through conifer plantation to begin with, and our first sight of anything other than fir trees was at Loch Caise: a pleasant spot, the path curving around one edge of the loch and then heading uphill through more conifers, and with a good display of cotton grass coming into flower at the loch edge.

On further until we once again came out on the open moorland at a cattle grid, where there was a trailer on which we sat to have our coffee break. Just as we arrived a skip lorry and another van turned up, with workmen who proceeded to load the skip with abandoned fencing wire and fence posts. One of the workers was happy to take a photo of all four of us on the trailer.

Passing another loch, and now no longer amid the forest, we kept on the track going uphill to reach another plantation, Strathmore Eileanach. After his absence yesterday, it was good to hear the cuckoo again as we walked through the wood.

As we reached the end of the wood we had our first sighting of Loch More: a large loch with a lovely curved sandy beach.

We walked along to the end of the Loch and then uphill on a stony track, with woodland on our right, until we reached the car park and our car.

Day 109   Monday 25th May 2015   Loch More to Loch Watten   13.4 miles

A wet start to the day, so we were all fully dressed in waterproofs when we started the walk from Loch More. It was also chilly, so hats and gloves on too. This was a bleak looking landscape of the Flow Country (blanket bog) and our route took us along a minor track before joining a 'B' road for most of the way across here.

There was a view back to the far distant mountains across the brown bog, and there was little in the way of landmarks to start with. However, we were accompanied on our way by song from the skylarks overhead, a pair of lapwings and the occasional curlew. Now and then we caught sight of red deer leaping across the otherwise seemingly deserted ground. We passed a small loch on our right and then some forestry but the scenery of the blanket bog was mainly unbroken. A few miles on we came to a large white house in an imposing position above the river and, nearby, a walled cemetery.

A bridge over a stream on our left was a pretty spot in the wilderness, with prolific displays of marsh marigolds in the stream beneath.

Keeping trekking onwards we arrived at Westerdale, aptly named, as it was a miniature Yorkshire Dales type scene, with the River Thurso tumbling dramatically over the rocks, and also from the mill leat, next to a picturesque stone built mill.

The sun had come out briefly here and we sat on the grassy mound by the river, and opposite the mill, to have our coffee. There were two impressive houses: one upstream of the mill and one downstream. It was quite incredible that such a 'green and pleasant oasis' should exist amongst the mainly desolate countryside around here.

Reluctantly we left this beautiful place and were soon out of Westerdale and walking through the flat flow

lands. Occasionally there were wind turbines in the otherwise featureless landscape, and we could just about see the distant mountains of the Highlands receding into the far distance.

The idyllic spot at Westerdale

We carried on now on the B870 to reach the A9 at Mybster. Crossing the A9 we continued on, and the countryside changed to more green fields and the occasional house dotted here and there. We found a spot, out of the strong wind, to have lunch. Sat against a flagstone wall near a small plantation of firs we had a view of men and machines putting in a fence line on the other side of the road.

As we approached Watten the scenery became more green, with pastureland, some small areas of woodland, some silver birch and some firs, and more frequent habitation. There were dry stone walls and then beech hedges lining the lane. We walked through Watten and shortly afterwards arrived at Loch Watten, and our waiting car.

Day 110 Saturday 23rd May 2015 Loch Watten to Killimster 7 miles

Having arrived at site at Bowermadder we decided to walk the 7 miles from Watten to Killimster. It was a lovely sunny day, and the men even decided to wear shorts: for the first time this holiday!

We left one car at Loch Watten, and walked along a lane until a footpath took us along a river bank. There were interesting stone walls, and it was very flat ground in the main.

Along the river bank were marsh marigolds and irises, not yet in flower. It was a pleasant walk with fields of cattle and sheep around us. Following the river we eventually came to gorse bushes; very scratchy and prickly, especially for those wearing shorts today; and the path then came out alongside a forestry plantation.

This we followed for a while, coming out onto a track past a farm and then on a lane crossing the railway at a level crossing. We carried on to a T Junction where we turned left along the B874 and walked for a while until we came to Bilbster Forest. Stopped here for a flapjack and a drink – unaware of the perils that were ahead!

On through the wood we came out on the other side of the plantation and onto the boggy moor of *Moss of Killimster:* aptly named (although I could now add other adjectives to describe this place.)

We made our way picking a path, trying to keep our feet dry as we went through reeds, irises, and heather interspersed with many kinds of boggy mossy mounds, until we reached a stream. This we had to cross, but it was too wide *and there was no bridge.*

We kept going, in a similar difficult manner as before, to make our way to a place to cross. This we did, and then we had a vast tract of boggy land to negotiate, keeping to the areas of heather where we could, as this was marginally less wet.

There was a very wet, and boggy, valley below us that we had to get across somehow and, in our aim to keep on the safer ground, we had to deviate from the most direct route.

How to get across this? we needed to reach the forest three miles away

By the time we'd reached the higher ground on the other side of this valley we all had wet, and cold, feet and wet boots. We had to keep going: the weather had changed since we set out and rain was arriving. Squelching our *very soggy* way across we finally made it to the bridge over the dyke that was mentioned in the guide book. This 'bridge' was, in fact, three logs with some rotten planks across only the middle section and with nails sticking out of the logs where, at some point in the bridge's past, planks had been. This was at least a change from bog and moss, and so we 'inched our way' across this 'bridge'. (Andy took photos as we ladies crossed this) From there it was more of the same bogginess to reach the

forest on the furthest side of the Moss. We followed the fence line to a cow field and then a farm track up to a lane where at last, and very thankfully, we were on dry ground and we made our way up to Killimster and our waiting car. Taking off our *extremely wet socks and bog-spattered boots* we decided a good plan of action was to drive into Wick and buy fish and chips for supper.

Back at site the boots and socks were washed, and put to dry! *(I think these three miles were the worst ground conditions that we've encountered since leaving Land's End.)*

Day 111 **Thursday 28ᵗʰ May 2015** **Killimster to Freswick Bay** **10.5 miles**

We left our car at Freswick, and took Bob's back to Killimster to start the walk. There was a cold fresh wind, and a forecast of heavy showers throughout the day. Once again we put on coats and hats. However, it was a relief that the Moss of Killimster was now behind us, and we had firm ground to walk on. We started along a lane to Reiss, where we could see the railway for the oil pipe line which runs dead straight for 5 miles. Along here we had sight of a small bird we didn't know. I took a photograph, and we think it is a wheatear.

At the Loch of Wester we crossed both the railway line and the Burn of Lyth, and then turned left onto the A99, briefly, before taking a right turn past a couple of fields and crossing a field to reach the sand dunes of Sinclair Bay. The sand dunes here were large and dramatic, and we made our way past these and down onto the lovely sandy beach.

Views from here to Ness Point and its lighthouse at the southern end of the bay. We walked north towards Keiss along the sands. Dexter had a great time fetching a large stick he found on the beach, and enjoyed crashing through the waves to retrieve it.

We passed a good display of wild flowers after leaving the harbour

At the end of Sinclair Bay we had to pick our way a bit across the stony shoreline to get along to Keiss Harbour.

Keiss Harbour

Along the shoreline were pill boxes from World War 2, and tank traps lined the upper shore. From one of the pill boxes we set up my camera to take a photo of all four of us (plus Dexter) as we neared the dramatic view of Keiss Castle in its prominent position on the rocky cliff top. The more modern and much larger Keiss Castle Hotel, inland from here, was impressive and better placed, but not so photogenic.

Unfortunately the cliff path now ran out: a real shame bearing in mind the number of people who walk Land's End to John O'Groats, and we had to make our way up to the A99. Fortunately it wasn't too busy, and there was a good wide grass verge to walk on too. There were frequent heavy and cold showers, some thunder later, although when the sun came out it was lovely.

We made a lunch stop at Helberry Harbour, where there was a high backed stone seat providing excellent shelter from the heavy shower that started just as we sat to have our lunch, and the harbour below us was very quaint: a real 'smuggler's cove'. There were beautiful displays of wild primroses growing on the cliff tops, and also some pink campion. Nearby was notice of Nybster Broch – an ancient dwelling place and a site of archaeological interest.

We returned to the A99 for a while, still having to keep our waterproofs on as the showers were now more frequent.

Then, later, leaving the A99 on a path down to the sea, we arrived at another castle: Freswick Castle situated in a pleasant location at the start of Freswick Bay. Making our way along to the end of the bay we then took a lane to reach our parked car at Freswick.

| Day 112 | Friday 29th May 2015 | Freswick to John O'Groats | 7 miles |

We awoke to a blue sky: we couldn't believe it after all the recent wet weather, and we set off happily to do the last section of the walk. On our drive to Freswick, to start the walk, we were amazed at the dramatic cloud formations low in the sky all around us, with blue sky above. It was lovely to see clear views and the countryside in the sunshine for the first time since we arrived a week ago.

Leaving our car at Freswick, where we'd finished yesterday, we walked along the lane toward the coast to Skirza, and then beyond on a good track through a farm. We then crossed to a track on the coastal moorland, with stunning views of blue sea.

A little further on we encountered our first 'geo' cliff formation at Skippie Geo. This was a vertiginous drop where many years ago a vast sea cave had collapsed, and there were seagulls nesting in every nook they could find. Sea pinks growing where they could made for an impressive view. On from there we followed a track near the cliff edge to pass and go round the even larger geo, Wife Geo, and on again to reach Fast Geo. Spectacular high cliffs at the geos and a home for many sea birds.

We then followed a path through heather moorland: some boggy sections, but not difficult, and were heading more inland for a while. From Burnt Hill there was a good track over the moor and there were suddenly views of the Orkney Islands, Stroma and the lighthouse at Duncansby Head.

Further on, to our left, we had our first sighting of the village of John O'Groats: with views still to the Orkney Islands, and to the north-east were the Stacks of Duncansby – great rock formations rising up from the sea and towering over the cliffs of the mainland. These were impressive and we had a coffee stop on the cliff tops, overlooking these amazing rock stacks.

The sun shone and, although there were clouds on the horizons, it stayed bright and clear all the way. We had hoped for a good final day's walk, and now our dreams were being realised and it was an amazing experience: especially as we had had very changeable, and often wet and cold, weather since we started walking in May this year. It was also a little strange to think we were finishing the walk after 1,441 miles of walking since we set out at Land's End in July 2011, and it was with mixed emotions that we made our way to the lighthouse at Duncansby Head, which is the actual furthest point north-east, and we were delighted to have a reception committee meet us there: Mike and Moreen Smith, with Pat and Michael Folkes. Mike had taken photos of us as we approached Duncansby Head, and I have included them in this log.

Our friends had been holidaying in Scotland and were camped at John O'Groats. We were photographed, and congratulated, before we were able to continue the mile or so to John O'Groats: the official end of the walk.

At the harbour our reception committee were there to meet us again: this time with a celebratory bottle of champagne. More photos at the signpost by the harbour as we celebrated.

We then had our LeJog Forms stamped officially, to authenticate our journey. We have to send these off to the Land's End to John O'Groats Association to get our certificates.

Pat and Michael, and Mike and Moreen, gave us a lift back to our car at Freswick and we then made our way to site at Bower. We were soon ready to make our journey south to Dingwall where we had managed at the last minute to get a pitch at the Camping and Caravanning Club Site. We have booked a meal at the National Hotel in Dingwall this evening to finish off the celebrations.

CONTENTS

Front Cover Photo: Meg, Andy and Dexter at Lochan an H-Earba
Walk Sections
How It All Came About
My View of the Walk
The first day photos

	Page Number
Section One: Land's End to Bath	
Land's End to Gulval Church	1
Gulval Church to Knave Go By	4
Knave Go By to Langarth	6
Langarth to Mitchell	8
Mitchell to St Wenn	10
St Wenn to Helland Bridge	12
Helland Bridge to Trebray	13
Trebray to Lifton	15
Lifton to Sourton	17
Sourton to Okehampton	19
Okehampton to Iddesleigh	21
Iddesleigh to Chittlehamholt	23
Chittlehamholt to Brayford	24
Brayford to Exford	26
Exford to Dunster	28
Dunster to West Quantoxhead	30
West Quantoxhead to North Petherton	32
North Petherton to Catcott	34
Catcott to Draycott	35
Draycott to Paulton	37
Paulton to **Bath**	39
Section Two: Bath to Chipping Campden	
Bath Abbey to Tormarton	42
Tormarton to North Nibley	44
North Nibley to Randwick Church	46
Randwick Church to Cooper's Hill	48
Cooper's Hill to Ham Hill	50
Ham Hill to Stanway	52
Stanway to **Chipping Campden**	54
Section Three: Chipping Campden to Malham Tarn	
Chipping Campden to Stratford Upon Avon	56
Stratford Upon Avon to Shrewley	58
Shrewley to Meriden	60
Meriden to Hurley	61
Hurley to Bucks Head Farm	62
Bucks Head Farm to beyond Lichfield	63
Lichfield to Rugeley	65
Rugeley to Uttoxeter	67
Uttoxeter to Blore	69
Blore to Hartington	71
Hartington to Miller's Dale	73
Miller's Dale to Upper Booth	76
Upper Booth to Torside	79
Torside Reservoir to near Redbrook Reservoir	80
Redbrook Reservoir to Blackstone Edge	81
Blackstone Edge to Clough Foot / Gorpal Reservoir	82

Clough Foot to Ponden Reservoir	84
Ponden to East Marton	85
East Marton to **Malham Tarn**	87

Section Four: Malham Tarn to Cow Green Reservoir

Malham Tarn to Horton in Ribblesdale	90
Horton in Ribblesdale to Hawes	92
Hawes to Keld	94
Keld to Bowes	96
Bowes to Middleton in Teesdale	99
Middleton in Teesdale to **Cow Green Reservoir**	101

Section Five: Cow Green Reservoir to the Falkirk Wheel

Cow Green Reservoir to Knock	104
Knock to Garrigill	106
Garrigill to Whitley Castle (Roman Fort)	108
Whitley Castle to Gilsland	110
Gilsland (Thirlwall Castle) to Housesteads	112
Housesteads to Bellingham	114
Bellingham to Byrness	116
Byrness to Windy Gyle (Cocklawfoot)	118
Cocklawfoot and Windy Gyle to Kirk Yetholm	120
Kirk Yetholm to Crailing	123
Crailing to Dryburgh Abbey	126
Dryburgh Abbey to Yair Bridge	128
Yair Bridge to Traquair	130
Traquair to White Meldon	133
White Meldon to beyond West Linton (Wakefield)	135
Wakefield to Lin's Mill Aqueduct	137
Lin's Mill Aqueduct to Linlithgow	140
Linlithgow to **The Falkirk Wheel**	141

Section Six: The Falkirk Wheel to Findhorn Bridge

The Falkirk Wheel to Kirkintilloch	143
Kirkintilloch to Milngavie	145
The West Highland Way	
Milngavie to Drymen	147
Drymen to Rowardennan	149
Rowardennan to Inverarnan	152
Inverarnan to Tyndrum	155
Tyndrum to Forest Lodge	157
Forest Lodge to Altnafeadh	159
Altnafeadh to Kinlochleven	161
Kinlochleven to Fort William	163
The East Highland Way	
Fort William to Spean Bridge	165
Spean Bridge to Inverlair	167
Inverlair to Moy Bridge	169
Moy Bridge to Pattack Falls	171
Pattack Falls to Newtonmore	173
Newtonmore to Ruthven Barracks	176
Ruthven Barracks to Kincraig	178
Kincraig to Aviemore *end of the East Highland Way*	181
Aviemore to near Carrbridge	184
Near Carrbridge to **Findhorn Bridge**	186

Section Seven: Findhorn Bridge to John O'Groats

Findhorn Bridge to Farr	187
Farr to Inverness	189
Inverness to Knockbain (Reelig Glen)	190
Knockbain to Ruisaurie	192
Ruisaurie to Marybank	194
Marybank to Dingwall	196
Dingwall to Evanton	198
Evanton to Ardross Church	200
Ardross Church to Wester Fearn	203
Wester Fearn to Loch Buidhe	205
Loch Buidhe to Golspie	207
Golspie to Brora	209
Brora to Lothbeg	211
Lothbeg to Kildonan	213
Kildonan to Forsinard	215
Forsinard to Altnabreac	217
Altnabreac to Loch More	219
Loch More to Loch Watten	220
Loch Watten to Killimster	222
Killimster to Freswick	224
Freswick to **John O'Groats**	227-231

Note: It will be noticed that the dates of the walk, in a few instances, are out of sequence and not continuous. Generally speaking, it was the weather which occasionally dictated a decision of this kind: for example, the walk from Hawes to Keld was postponed until the weather was suitable for ascending the higher fells.

Other days: when we had moved site in the morning, it made sense to take advantage of the afternoon to walk a shorter distance: not necessarily the next consecutive section.

When Bob had the injury to his leg on the final section of the walk, we had several days without walking, and it was felt necessary to walk the short section from Brora to Lothbeg out of sequence, to ascertain if Bob was fit to continue.

Our aim of a continuous walk of seven sections to reach our goal has, in the main, been achieved.

Land's End, Cornwall

John O' Groats. (Orkney Isles in the distance)